STEAMPUNK MASHUP

ALSO BY BILL LYNAM

Footloose Pilgrims: A Journal of Moped Travels through Europe (2014)
in collaboration with Dick Lynam

STEAMPUNK MASHUP

A Collection of Victorian Adventures

Bill Lynam

PUYUP PUBLISHING
Prescott, Arizona
2017

First Edition

Library of Congress Control Number: 2017935273

ISBN 978-0-9912574-0-9

Printed in the United States of America

Puyup Publishing Company
4875 Comanche Trail
Prescott, AZ 86301

Acknowledgements

The idea for this book came from a creative writing class I took from Kristen Kauffman at Yavapai College in Prescott, Arizona. Her enthusiasm for this relatively young genre was new, catching, and fun to explore.

Russ Miller's sketches visualize characters as they experience a critical moment. His fine hand explodes them into action by pencil.

As always, my thanks to all the readers, editors, and technical assistants who framed this work. Patrick Fogarty suggested critical online software and gave valuable feedback; Terry Lund for her insightful reading and commentary; Jennifer Longworth for assembly and feedback of the works; and my wife Maria, for her patience, many contributions, and editorial expertise.

for Maria Ann Lynam

and in memory of Kyle Evan Lynam, Sr.
1974 to 2002

Contents

ILLUSTRATIONS

PREFACE

STEAMPUNK: A subgenre of science fiction and fantasy, incorporates technology and aesthetic designs inspired by 19TH century industrial steam-powered machinery. It is accompanied by mad science, airships, strange chemistry, horror, and neo-Victorian aesthetics.

The steampunk genre is enjoying a vogue in many areas, particularly in visual arts, design, literature, and other fields where it has come to influence and change ways of looking at common objects. It has sparked the imagination with the concept of taking something old or unusual and melding it with the new, transforming it into something else or fantastic, or un-thought of, including something campy, kitschy, or punky.

There is an emphasis on steam in these stories because the industrial age had an impact on replacing animal, wind, water, and human manual labor with machines and mass production. Although many of the stories here have steam in them, some do not, but they do give allegiance to the imaginative realm of steampunk and fantasy.

STEAMPUNK MASHUP

DANNY

DANNY JUMPED SHIP in Bournemouth, England and made his way to London on a stagecoach. He was on his quest to see the queen, a desire he'd nurtured ever since he'd heard about the Kohinoor Diamond and how the queen was the only one who'd wear it because of its curse. He wanted to see the queen and the diamond.

Unfortunately, his coach to London was held up en route by highwaymen and everyone lost their shillings but him. When the men on horse shouted, "Stand and deliver your purse," Danny had a ruse. His purloined fob watch had two knobs, one for winding the regular internal time mechanism and a second that put him into the blue zone, as he liked to call it. This was an altered state of time that only lasted for an hour or so—just time enough to do many interesting things.

The watch came into his hands by his usual trade—he filched by slight-of-hand whatever came his way. When walking towards what appeared to be a well-off gentleman, Danny saw the gent's watch. Attracted by its shiny gold surface and its size, he nudged him and glanced off him as though he was drunk. Danny was sufficiently coordinated to excuse himself and kept on going with his prize in hand. The gentleman adjusted his ruffled torso, picked up his dislodged hat, and with a mild curse for the drunk, kept on going, unaware of being lighter than before.

Initially, Danny took the watch to a pawn shop in his hometown, Halifax, Nova Scotia, Canada and tried to sell it either as a watch or for its gold content. The shopkeeper looked at Danny and said, "Let me see it," in an entrusting way. Danny thought the man seemed very eager to get his hands on the piece, much too eager. Immediately suspicious, Danny countered with, "On the other hand, I think I'll keep it." That was when the shopkeeper came around the counter and went to the door and shouted for the local constable standing on the corner, "I've a thief here, come and catch him."

Danny bowled past the shopkeeper, narrowly escaping being grabbed by the collar, and ran out of the shop and high-tailed it without being followed. When he slowed down, he dodged into a pub. Sauntering up to the bar, he asked for a pint. The bartender pulled a draft from the engine and held it until Danny could produce a pence to pay for it.

"Might young, aren't you?" The barkeep said.

"No, I just look young for me age," Danny quipped, as he hoisted the ale and tossed it off.

Back at his lodgings, he looked over the watch. He wound up the regular stem and saw it worked well. Curious about the other knob, he pressed it and time seemed to stand still. Or, maybe it didn't—holding onto the watch, he walked around outside and everything around him was silent, still and unmoving. The horses stood immobile, the people were stopped in their tracks, with no clatter of hooves on the cobblestones, all as quiet as a cemetery at midnight, conversations were absent, and he could walk up to people and they wouldn't budge.

To give it a test, he lifted a gent's wallet and walked around the corner. No alarm, no noise came from the guy, he just stood still along with everyone around him. Danny decided he'd gone into some kind of time warp where he was faster than anyone he knew. He confirmed it when he pressed the button again, everybody and everything started moving again and kept on going as though nothing had happened.

Danny went back to his room after his test and pondered his new toy. This watch is better than gold, he thought. He knew that Halifax was too small a town to use the watch too often. It could be dangerous and he could come under suspicion if he relieved too many people of their fortunes. He knew it would help him to leave Nova Scotia sooner than he planned.

Danny, a farm boy from Winnipeg, Manitoba had run away from home and wanted to go to Great Britain. How he was going to get there, he had no idea. He always described his goal as going to see the queen. After that, he had no idea what he was going to do. The adventure of getting to England was all he needed to keep going. Now with the watch, he had the means for a steamer ticket.

On board ship, he used all the watch's secrets to his advantage. Hungry all the time, he'd go into the dining area, hit the blue zone button on the watch in his pocket and all the passengers in the dining room stopped whatever they were doing. Then Danny would stroll in, grab a plate and sit down and eat. When done, he'd leave the hall, hit the blue button and everything returned to normal, leaving behind some perplexed passengers with empty dinner plates where he had eaten their food.

So, when the highwaymen halted his stagecoach to London, he hit the blue zone button and picked the pockets of his fellow travelers, then exited the carriage and took the highwaymen's watches, and money. Then he prowled their saddle bags for all their loot. He disappeared behind some high rocks and peeked over and hit the blue button again. The robbers kept at their business but could not figure out why all the passengers were broke. Frustrated, they rode off with anything they could find in the passenger's luggage, which wasn't that much, and unaware of their own plight.

When the highwaymen moved on and the stagecoach continued the journey to London, Danny came out of hiding and hiked to the nearest town–Southampton. He found the railway station and waited for the next train to London. When it came, he helped a crippled woman onto the train by carrying her luggage, then proceeded to stow away for a while. When the train got underway, he found a seat and pretended to read a newspaper until he heard the conductor coming

down the aisle. Casually, he hit the blue button, palmed a ticket stub from the luggage rack above a passenger in a forward car, then returned to his seat in his own carriage, and put the stub above it, and reset time by hitting the blue button. Danny relaxed, a fully, paid-up, ticketed passenger.

In London, he teamed up with a boy who put him in touch with a fence and turned his loot from the stagecoach into pounds sterling. Finding lodging, he could now proceed to his mission to see the queen, who he hoped might be wearing the huge diamond.

Danny saw a copy of *The Illustrated London News*. It showed a picture of Queen Victoria and Prince Albert in an open carriage on their weekly jaunt through Queen's Gate to Hyde Park, a ritual they kept to when there were no official gatherings to attend and it wasn't raining. They were accompanied by the coach driver and a footman, with the Queen's mounted Life Guard trailing behind.

In the accompanying article, the reporter mentioned that the queen had been accosted and shot at over seven times. She had also once been attacked by a Fenian wielding a shillelagh, who caused no serious harm to the royal person. The article recited the attempts on her life and her endurance through all of them. One story even mentioned that she went back to the park the day after an attempt to give her would-be assassin another shot at her. The shooter returned, as well. The police lured him out and arrested him when he tried again.

Danny, enthralled with the idea of seeing the queen, decided to hang out in Hyde Park along the queen's route. He spent a lot of useless time there. But one Wednesday at three o'clock he was rewarded. Positioned in the park, he saw the royal carriage with Queen Victoria and Prince Albert coming along the path. He also noted someone partially concealed in the bushes nearby. Danny remained out of sight and kept an eye on the other fellow as the coach pulled abreast. The person hiding stepped out with a pistol and aimed it at the royal personage.

Danny hit the blue button, walked over to the would-be assassin and took his pistol. Going back to the trailing Queen's Guard, he took out his jackknife and cut portions of the reins from several of the mounted horsemen. With these, he then went back to the accoster and trussed him hand and foot and threw him back into the bushes. That done, he walked up to the carriage and said hello to the Queen and her consort. He noted she was not wearing the diamond that day. Since the royal couple were mute, whatever Danny said didn't register but he was satisfied. He'd met the Queen on his terms. He walked safely away before hitting the blue button to return everything to normal. The royal carriage trundled on followed by the Queen's Life Guards.

Exiting the park and walking down Bayswater Road, Danny mentioned to a bobby he met that he saw a body lying in the bushes along the carriage path in Hyde Park and perhaps, he should investigate.

Pleased with himself, Danny knew he had saved the queen from her ninth assassination attempt. As for the diamond, he went to see the Kohinoor in the Tower of London where it was kept on display. The display case retold the 14th century curse:

"He who owns this diamond will own the world, but will also know all its misfortunes. Only God, or a woman, can wear it with impunity."

THE EXPERIMENT

AS THE SCIENCE WRITER for the Boston Globe, I was sent to report on a conference in Paris. The paper paid my way but not very generously. My berth in steerage on the *S.S. La Gascogne* and the food in third class proved disgusting. Arriving in Paris, I connected with other journalists, and we found a pied-a-terre on the *Rive Gauche* for a few *sou* and split the rent.

My editor sent me because he thought I could speak French since I had taken some in high school. I knew better and hired Jacques Marchand, who offered himself as a translator. When I spoke with him, he said he had no difficulty understanding or translating scientific jargon. Over a *vin ordinaire*, he mentioned he'd been expelled from the University of Paris, the Sorbonne. His peccadillo and the price for it came from organizing a protest march on the university and occupying the president's office as a rally against capitalism and consumerism. Over 500 students helped him occupy the building resulting in the closing of the university for the first time in 700 years. He smirked a little as he gleefully reminisced on his coup d'état.

At the opening of *La Conference Scientifique Internationale de 1890*, Jacques and I viewed the exhibits and received the conference program. One presentation in particular, caught my eye. Oliver Wendell Holmes, the American inventor who popularized the stereoscope, would speak about an exploration tool never before tried. He would also conduct an experiment to determine whether the combined tools would prove their usefulness or not. Scheduled to take place at a village 30 kilometers outside of Paris on the following Monday, meant we had to be there to observe and subsequently write my article.

Jacques and I sought out Holmes.

"What does this new device of yours do and what can be its utility?" I asked.

"You can tell your Boston readers this machine is better than baked beans. It has the potential of finding deposits of natural, but useful metals like cobalt, iron, nickel, and also rare metals," Holmes replied.

"But, how does it work?" I persisted.

"Come to the demonstration! You can fly with me and see for yourself. Be on the north side of Evry, south of Paris on Monday at nine. You will be amazed," Holmes exclaimed. "Attend this afternoon's lecture first, so you'll understand more about the device before we demonstrate it."

At the lecture we listened to Dr. Holmes, who spoke passable French according to Jacques. We sought a copy of the lecture from Holmes afterward, so I could use it to write an article for the *Globe*. Although in French, I had Jacques translate it.

Holmes was testing an improved magnetometer coupled to a battery-driven self-writing machine, an autoscript, installed in a dirigible. When it passed over the terrain, magnetic anomalies record on Hachure Maps. The autoscript records the magnetometer's signals on maps in their relative earth position. A cartographer substitutes appropriate maps of the terrain as the location changes.

Every ferromagnetic mineral has a unique signal or signature when monitored, just like people have unique fingerprints. Previous lab tests established each mineral's signature. Holmes expected signatures previously detected on the ground should be similar to those recorded from the air. He was testing to see if it would work at all and what was the best altitude for each mineral.

A reporter for *France Soir* interrupted Holmes' lecture and barked, "There are no significant iron mines in France except the Lorraine, so what good is it? We already know what's there. How could you positively discover anything with your contraption way up in the air, anyway?"

"Quite easily," Holmes replied, "we'll be using ingots of the metals we want to test. This experiment is not just for France alone, but the whole world," he proclaimed.

On Monday, Jacques and I found the field in Evry after a long stagecoach ride. Sitting in the middle of the field was a gigantic balloon with hand-cranked propellers protruding from each end of a large wicker basket. A large steering vane or rudder that could swing and change the dirigible's direction of flight was attached below the stern of the basket. This whole apparatus sat amid hay bales on someone's farmland. Jacques took one look at the airship and said, "I leave it to the birds to fly. I'll be watching you up there from this solid little patch of earth. Have a fantastic flight."

I didn't blame Jacques for his lack of enthusiasm to become birdlike. Nevertheless, I'd come a long way and needed a story. I left him to take pictures of our flight with a folding Rochester camera loaded with roll-film the newspaper had entrusted to me. Then I was ready for this merry ride.

A fireman tending a furnace situated on a slate floor in the basket provided hot air for the balloon. The balloon rose slightly, and the crew hurried to secure the airship's tie-downs before lift-off.

The Cosmological Signature Detector or CSD, as Holmes called his magnetometer, was ready with its long cables coiled. Its sensing bar magnet dangled at the end of the wire. Once aloft, the experiment would start with its unreeling.

Guarded by the gendarmerie so the peasants wouldn't steal them, bundles of iron bars sprinkled one field. In other nearby fields, bars of nickel and cobalt were arrayed in their plots and also guarded. Other magnetic minerals are relatively rare and not found in great concentrations, so were not part of the experiment.

Preparing to go aloft, two men cranked the propellers at each end of the dirigible at the captain's command, while the fireman kept the hot air flowing to the balloon. The cartographer readied the CSD. Holmes fetched me and once aboard, I was told to stay out of the crew's way. The captain steered the ship and Holmes ran the experiment.

Once airborne, the captain ascended to 1,000 feet according to his altimeter, then tried to hold the airship steady at that altitude, while Holmes began his experiment. Once that elevation was reached, Holmes told the cartographer to activate the CSD and reeled out the long CSD cable to within 100 feet of the ground. The first of ten passes over the metal ingots at 100-foot intervals at increasing distances from the ground had begun. After each pass, the coil was ratcheted up a hundred feet for the next pass. Below, the tip of the cable held the sensing bar magnet that flew like a stinger on a bug looking for its prey.

The captain steered the airship and fought to keep it at the 1,000-foot elevation above the ground. The winds pushed us around and the propeller men cranked at his command.

Strokes appeared on the Hachure Map as the captain told the crew to steer over the iron bars on the first field. A flurry of impressions flew from the autoscript, identifying the iron imprint when the magnet was over the deposit, then changing as the craft flew beyond. When the airship passed over the cobalt and nickel stacks, notations were produced on maps at their deposit locations. Holmes reeled the CSD up the prescribed amount to gather more signatures from the deposits. As the CSD magnet got higher, the signals faded and became less effective.

"Thunderation, this is some pumpkins," Holmes shouted, as he watched the squiggles and saw they matched the ground sample signatures for each metal. As the flight passes continued over the metals at different altitudes, it soon became obvious that iron (FE) had the highest magnetic moment and signature at the highest altitude, Cobalt (CO) the next lowest moment and a better signature at lower altitudes. Nickel (NI) the least moment and needed the lowest height to be

detected.

My telegraphed copy of this wondrous experiment made the headlines of *The Boston Globe* back home. The scientific community applauded this serendipitous moment of discovery. New England scientists immediately began to prepare to replicate the experiment, building their own airborne detector sets to search for minerals in the Americas.

Jacques and I had a rousing send-off at a local bistro on the docks at the Port of Le Havre.

"Luke, *mon ami*, we shall be friends forever. When I finish at the university, I'll come to America to see and understand about your democracy. After all, my people helped save your country," Jacques said.

I returned to Boston, but this time in second class as I had cabled my editor "no more steerage." When the developed roll-film from the folding Rochester camera arrived at the newspaper, there were several shots of the dirigible. One showed it on the ground, two in the air and a fuzzy one as it passed overhead. Of the hundred frames in the camera, most were shots of a cute barmaid and various customers in the wine shop near the field at Evry. Jacques warned me about this as I prepared to depart for home. He said everybody in the bar wanted their picture taken and for every picture he took, he received a shot of vino. I remembered when he gave me the camera back after we landed, he was goofy and weaving.

As a gesture of Franco-American goodwill, I packaged the bar photos and sent them to the Mayor of Evry to submit to the local bar owner for his customers.

FOSSICKING

J, AN AUSTRALIAN immigrant without papers, jumped ship in the harbor of San Pedro, California. He had been shanghaied in Melbourne, Australia to crew the *Balclutha*; a triple-masted, steel-hulled, full-rigged ship, it traded Aussie coal for northwest timber out of San Francisco. A jackaroo or ranch hand on a cattle station, J had come to Melbourne for a weekend off. After too many schooners of Australian beer and a Mickey Finn, he woke to find out he had a new profession—sailor.

Besides looking for work in the San Pedro and Los Angeles area, J walked the beach in his spare time, fossicking the surf and the high tide line for any interesting flotsam, jetsam, or lagan he could find. He meandered for miles along the shore where the sea and waves had pounded out undercut banks and enclaves, looking for any treasure. Several tunneled promontories appeared to be arches or cave-like passages but were only seafront cut through by the surf. He would walk into these dim recesses to see if there was anything to scrounge, then he'd walk out the other side and continue down the beach.

He contemplated whether burglars had hidden stolen goods in any of these spots. He would ponder whether someone had lost something of value, like a diamond or gold ring loosened by seawater, or perhaps, someone had dropped a coin or two. Mostly, what he found were Japanese glass fishing-net ball floats, some with netting still attached, or pieces of a shipwreck that came ashore. Occasionally he would discover

a pair of spectacles, ripped off someone's nose when they stumbled while swimming.

One of his prizes was a life-buoy with the name of the sailing vessel–*Hoodoo*–that had grounded on a reef off Port Hueneme in 1888 and broken up. He'd gone to *The Los Angeles Herald* and in the newspaper's morgue found the details on the ship's grounding. That was his sweetest find to date.

Stepping over some rocks, he tripped slightly, then felt a sharp pain on his bare left foot. He looked down and saw he was bleeding on the sand. Quickly, he ran down to the water's edge and washed his foot in the saltwater, then hobble-hopped to a large rock, sat and bound his foot with a kerchief. With the bleeding stopped, he walked back to where he was injured to see what he'd stepped on. It wasn't a sharp rock, but rather, a spike or what looked like a big nail. Something that didn't belong there. He started to dig it up so no one else would get hurt. The more he dug, the more the thing grew. Excavating, he uncovered a spike on the top of a metal object. First digging with his hands until they got sore, he then found a piece of driftwood to make a digging stick. When he'd gotten a good chunk of sand away from the thing, he started pulling, trying to wrest it from the ground, but it wouldn't give. Digging some more, he finally had his prize an hour later. It was a funny looking helmet.

Lifting it out of the ground, he dumped out the sand inside it, took it down to the surf and washed it. Swishing it back and forth in the water, the sand loosened and it cleaned itself. The helmet appeared to be bronze or a similar kind of metal. It was fairly thick with a three-inch spike on its crown. Metal protuberances reminiscent of cow horns stuck out on either side and there were plates on the back and front. The front plate had slits to see through.

After he brought it home and looked it over, he found some strange symbols around the top of the helmet. They were in a language he didn't understand. Incised in the metal in cuneiform or wedge-like indentations, the marks looked like letters, but others seemed to be more like decorative squiggles. They were strange, foreign, unlike anything he'd seen before. It was like they were trying to tell a story—one he couldn't decipher.

Out of curiosity, he put it on his head, and it fit perfectly. Soon he began to feel differently, as though he'd become a warrior or something—another person, someone important. "Blewdy 'ell, that's bonsa," he exclaimed, "this thing's got power!" When he took it off, J returned to his normal, inquisitive self.

He decided to take it to the teacher's college and see if they knew what the symbols meant. Directed to the language department, they copied the symbols and said they'd get in touch with him when they figured them out. They thought they looked like runes, Old Norse characters, or maybe they were just scratches.

Two months later, he received a letter that said the college had been unable to translate the marks or whatever the squiggles were. They thought they were runes and had sent a copy of them to a university in Norway, Det Kongelige Frederiks Universitet in Oslo, for translation.

The local consensus figured it had something to do with the Scandinavian culture, but they were not sure which one. A return letter from Oslo arrived with an explanation of the marks. It was in Norwegian. The college's language department, heavy on Spanish speakers but no Nordic language speakers, said they had to find someone to translate it. When they did, they would be in contact with him.

J went to the school and took a look at the letter out of curiosity. One of the professors pointed out in the correspondence where it had the translation of the marks or whatever it was but said she could not read it herself. It spelled:

Denne hjelmen til hoerer, Ragnar fyrste--Jytland, drapsmann av Erwich, oedeleggenen av Eiger. Han som eier denne hjelmen vil vet han trenger a vite og ma bruke det gode og ikke det ande eller Loki vil sla du.

So much for that J thought, he only spoke Australian. He copied the letter's translation in pencil in case he ran into a Norseman who could do the job before the school did.

Back home, J put on the helmet thinking maybe something might happen, as before. He took out the letter and started reading it as if talking to a mate. Of course, he didn't understand the words but sounded them out. As he read the scramble of letters, they started to make sense in his head. The helmet was translating for him and telling him what the helmet scratches meant.

The translation came to him as he read the words:

This helmet belongs to Ragnar, Prince of Jutland, slayer of Erwich, destroyer of Eigger. He who owns this helmet will know all he needs to know and must use it for good and not evil or Loki will smite you.

"Crikey," J exclaimed, "this thing is fair dinkum all right. I wonder how else I can use it." It spoke to him in English so it wasn't restricted to the Norwegian language. And, it said the helmet had power. It also said bad things could happen if misused. He had some things to figure out about his new find.

Several months later, the teacher's college sent a letter to J with a translation of the Norwegian letter they received in English. They said the inscriptions were a form of proto-Norse runes, and their translation from Norwegian, a fair representation of the one he'd received from the helmet.

THE CURSE

THE TOWER GUARDS known as Beefeaters knew Queen Victoria occasionally ordered one jewel or another to be brought to her. She loved wearing them, and the most expensive resided in the Tower. Affairs of state demanded she deck herself out with the riches of the Empire. After all, as the Queen of Great Britain and all its dominions: Canada, Ireland, India, Australia, and many others, it was expected that she wear the royal patrimony.

"Blimey! The gem's gone again," the Yeoman Sergeant of the Guard announced as he took inventory of all the gems in the Tower, as per his duty. Concerned, he rang up the colonel and reported the missing diamond.

"It's all right sergeant, we know where it is. I have her chit here at headquarters. She signed out the *Koh* for the Royal Ascot races. It'll be back in a few days now that the races are over."

Jewel orders came from Buckingham Palace via telegraph in code so they knew it came from her Highness. The Kohinoor had been out of the Tower for a few weeks, which raised concern. Although its value has never been appraised, at 105.60carats, comparable in size to the Cullinan Diamond, its probable worth was in the millions of pounds sterling.

The colonel appeared at ease about it, though he had begun to worry about the jewel. This unique diamond was not entirely safe in the queen's boudoir. Although Queen Victoria might be the Empress of India, there were sore losers out there. The East India Company had seized the stone from the Indians in 1877. The Indians were not happy about losing the diamond, even though it had a curse on it.

The curse went:

"He who owns this diamond will own the world, but he will also know all its misfortunes. Only God, or a woman, can wear it with impunity."

The East Indians, the Persians, and the Afghanis, had all owned the sparkler at one time or another. They were clamoring for the diamond's return and were not averse to stealing it back given the opportunity.

While the Beefeaters were pondering the whereabouts of the jewel, Drina (Victoria's nickname from her full name: Alexandrina Victoria), was visiting her favorite aunt in Hanover, Germany. Prince Albert stayed home and now had an opportunity to indulge in one of his favorite recreations. Alone in his wife's dressing room, Albert began his secret ritual.

Taking his clothes off, he stood naked before the floor mirror admiring himself. Then he walked to the queen's wardrobe and began to dress. Cross-dressing was his pleasure and mischief. He pulled out a dresser drawer and extracted knee-high black silk stockings and carefully drew them on one at a time. From another drawer, he found cotton drawers with two overlapping flaps and donned them. From her closet, he chose a sleeveless, knee-length chemise and slipped it on. Back to the closet, he found a whalebone corset with garters. He cinched the garment in front; it almost took his breath away, it was so tight. He loved the way it seemed to compress about four inches of his belly, making him look slim and youthful.

Gliding to the floor length mirror, he admired his partial attire and inhaled the queen's perfume that lingered on her clothing. It excited him, and he sailed over to her vanity and sought out her favorite perfume concocted by her perfumery, Gutterson House—*Fleur de Bulgarie*. He generously spritzed himself with it and continued his search.

By the closet, he found a flexible bell-shaped crinoline and put it on. A camisole slid over the corset and then a simple petticoat, over which he swirled an elaborately embroidered petticoat with Saxe-Coburg and Gotha Heraldry symbols on the hem. A gift from him to Drina, he had made especially for her.

A royal gown with tiny iridescent pearls and Bohemian garnets sprinkled throughout was his wife's newest acquisition. It had long sleeves and a high neck. The fastenings were in the back and difficult to reach. Without a lady's maid, he did his best. It didn't bother him as he would not be wearing the garment long and certainly not in public.

Almost done, he strolled to the closet and opened another dresser for gloves to match the dress. It was too bad he couldn't fit into her ballroom slippers. He skipped the hat boxes—he wasn't going out. But he did want to see how the ermine cape looked atop his garments.

He always waited until the last piece of the ensemble was adjusted to see how the outfit looked. He loved the smell of her clothes and the frisson of wearing them. Pirouetting in front of the pier mirror, he thought the combination not quite right. He went to her jewel box and took out the chunky diamond she favored. What a rock! Over a hundred carats. He took it to the window to enjoy its scintillation. And, he'd had a hand in an attempt to increase its brilliance by having it cut in an oval shape in the Netherlands down from 186 carts to its present size. The result was not what he expected but he still loved the stone.

The pale afternoon sun poked through the coal fire smoke over London. The sky dimmed with a gray fuggy light and a malodorous nose. Twisting the diamond in his hand to catch the darkling light, the jewel stayed listless, hardly refracting. Nevertheless, he thought it added allure to his borrowed costume, and he fondled it. Knowing its bloody history and its curse, he enjoyed the luster of the jewel on his skin. He lit a cigar, poured himself a dollop of his favorite scotch, single-malt Islay Bunnahabhain, and settled in his favorite armchair. He savored the illusion of sliding over to the feminine side, the superb Sumatra

tobacco, the smoky peat taste of the liquor, and Drina's brief absence. After an interval of luxuriating in the garments, fondling the sensuous fabrics, it became time to replace them in the royal wardrobe. Putting the jewel back in its box, he decided to go riding.

That night, Albert called for the palace physician. "*Ich habe krank werden* (I'm ill), do you have a curative for me?" he stammered in poor English when the doctor arrived.

"Certainly," Sir William Gull said, "let's see what your symptoms are. It's a mystery why you've been taken ill so quickly. No one else in the palace is sick."

"Do you think it's serious?" the prince consort queried.

"Not likely. But, we'll find out. We have to expunge the bad blood." Gull proceeded to bleed a liter of blood from the prince's left arm.

"I'm woozy, and I can't see very well. Things look dark," the prince said, after he'd been bled.

"Now does it hurt any particular place?" the doctor asked.

"Mostly my head, like someone with little hammers is pounding inside my skull."

"Rest now, but before you do, I also have a cathartic for you." The physician rooted around in his black bag and extracted a purgative concoction. He'd received it from a Chinese friend, who said it worked every time. He recalled Dr. Chin say it contained peach kernel, rhubarb soaked in gin, mountain root, bitter orange and a dram of mirabilite. Pouring a jigger of the concoction into a glass, he added a shot of laudanum and a measure of whiskey to improve the bad taste. He gave it to the prince to drink.

"That'll cure your symptoms, prince. See you in the morning. Be sure you have a clear path to the loo, you'll soon be getting a reaction. Guten Nacht," Gull said as he left the room to his mostly German speaking patient.

The next morning, Prince Albert was found by the physician sweating profusely, the bed sheets fouled. The servants were called to clean him up and change the bed clothing.

"Would you like something to eat, your Highness?" the doctor asked.

"Nein, Nein, just kill me. What was in that drink you gave me? I feel like my insides are being boiled in oil," Albert complained.

"Now, now, we are only trying to cure you." the doctor soothed.

"Doctor, bitte, ablassen! I don't think I'll last through another of your cures. I have an idea of what ails me. But, you can't discuss it with anyone. Ja?"

"Certainly, your Highness, you can tell me anything."

"I tried on the queen's Kohinoor diamond just to see how it looks. I know it has a curse on it; particularly, if a man should own or wear it. I wonder if that is what made me ill? I don't believe in curses, but just maybe, eh?" he confided.

"Prince Albert, I have an idea. A colleague of mine is in town, Dr. Akito Jamoto, an orthopath. He just arrived from Greece and told me about a marvelous cure he discovered there. He's in town for a fortnight, and I will summon him."

"Anything doctor, but hurry. My head is starting to pound again."

Gull told a servant to bring Jamoto to the palace quickly along with his kit and miraculous curative.

When Dr. Jamoto arrived, he instructed Dr. Gull to set up a pan over a Bunsen burner. Then he warmed his wondrous ingredients into a liquid compound. When the solution cooled, he loaded the aesculapian elixir into a syringe and instructed Prince Albert to roll over and expose his buttocks. With a quick movement, he inserted the needle in a cheek and depressed the plunger, unloading the contents of the barrel. Twenty-four hours later, the prince was himself again.

When Drina returned from Germany, the prince suggested it might be a good idea to get the Kohinoor diamond back into the Tower of London.

"The tourists might want to see it," he suggested.

THE DUELLO

DOC HOLIDAY SAUNTERED over to the Palace Bar in Prescott, Arizona where he was banking the Faro table. When he left his hotel, his boots were freshly waxed by the bootblack in the hotel foyer. The handmade boots from top grade cowhide in Maryland were incised with his family motto: *Quarta Saluti* (Fourth Greetings). In the short walk to the saloon through the monsoon rain-muddied passageways of Montezuma Street, soil from horse manure, chewing tobacco spittle, roiled and wetted earth and tossed garbage smeared his footwear so that they looked like any cowboy's dusty, mud-entrenched foot coverings. He used the boot scraper at the entrance at the saloon's door to get the dough-like, congealing mess off before entering,

Walking up to the bar, he ordered a bourbon neat and proceeded to his Faro table. Doc's dapper figure had been confounded by fits of consumption; racking coughs left him thin, almost emaciated. His symptoms were kept at bay with whiskey and laudanum. He took out a small bottle of tincture of opium and splashed a dollop into his whiskey glass. The opium kept his coughing in check while the whiskey killed the tincture's lousy taste.

Jack, his case keeper, had the cards laid out and set on the table, all thirteen spades arranged for the customers to lay off their bets up to the house limit. Jack ran the abacus-like casekeep to help the punters keep track of their bets. They were betting against the deck in the dealing box. Doc banked the game today, using his own specially made two-card, gaffed dealing box. Instead of one card, it released two when he wished, one of which he palmed off. It gave him more than a slight edge in any game.

"Where's Timmy?" Doc asked. "He should have been here an hour ago." Waiting for an answer from Jack, Doc adjusted the gold stickpin in his tie. It had a Cripple Creek gold nugget soldered on the tip with a small carved walrus ivory seal head with diamond eyes.

"He's sick boss. His kid came by and said he couldn't make it tonight. Probably two sheets, for all I know."

"Well, we'll need another lookout. Get ahold of one of the Earp brothers. They're good. See if you can find Morgan. You got your abacus all warmed up, Jack?"

"Certainly, boss," Jack replied. "I'll go down to the Bird Cage; Morgan hangs out there."

Doc twirled the ring on his pinkie, an old mine cut diamond set in a gold ring he'd cast with his dental tools. The gold was from his Colorado adventures. On his other hand, he wore another gold ring with three semi-matched longitudinal gold nuggets stitched across the top. One of the nuggets had a chip missing, the result of a bar fight. Given Doc's slight build, he more often relied on his guns than his fists. His heavily tooled holster sported a Colt Single Action Army .45, not to mention his Remington .41 caliber Double Derringer he carried in his pocket and a five-inch knife in his boot scabbard

That night Doc dealt. He'd left Kate Harony, his sometime girlfriend, known as Big Nose Kate, back at the hotel. She didn't want to sit around the bar and watch a bunch of drunks roaring over their winnings, or more likely their losses, since Doc was manipulating the cards.

As the card games began, more local cowboys and ranchers strolled into the Palace Bar. They'd heard Doc Holiday had hit town. His reputation followed him. They whispered he'd shoot before he would discuss it if someone disputed him. Only twenty-nine, he'd wounded or killed several card players over disputes. He also had a reputation for beating up his foes with his walking stick. Some were eager to go up against him in cards but were careful not to provoke him given his notoriety. Cross the man and you could wind up in boot hill, they said.

Others came wandering in just to watch, but they had to sit at the bar. Sitting at the bar, though, was no free show. You had to drink. Let your glass sit too long, and you'd find a fresh glass with a new shot of whiskey in it with the bartender giving you the pay-up or get out look. No one was allowed to just sit or have an empty glass or idle whiskey.

After a half hour of play with Doc dealing all the cards for another round, one of the players, a local cowhand, Dilley Browne, had lost his wages and called Doc on his dealing.

Dilley, a cowpuncher and farmer, liked to shoot his mouth off on just about anything. People who knew him let it pass. He just had a lot of wind to get out of his system, they said. What Dilley didn't know about Doc and his highly sensitive nature, would not be helping him that night. Doc didn't let the slightest affront go unchallenged.

Dilley, a year older than Doc, wore a ragged, sweat-stained cowboy hat that was a little too small for his big head. His hay bale arms were loaded with freckles and he wore bib overalls that looked to be his only pair. He was one of six brothers and they all worked the family's hardscrabble farm. They'd cleared the bush and trees on unclaimed land and built the barns, sheds and a house where they lived together. Dilley was in town to have a little fun that Saturday night.

"Looks like you drew two cards instead of one but only one card surfaced when you dealt from the box," Dilley said.

Doc looked at him and said, "Farmboy, you think I'm cheating? 'Cause that's what you're saying." Then Doc emptied the box of the remaining cards and shoved it over to the cowpoke with a fresh deck of cards. "If you know how this thing works, show me."

Dilley got up and ambled over to the Faro box and looked inside, then all over the outside. He pawed the inside some more to see if there was any contraption or spring that shouldn't be there. Then, he loaded it with a fresh deck of cards and dealt. Only one card came out. He dealt again and still only one card came out. He did it several more times with the same result. He never found Doc's pressure plate that ejected two cards at once when the correct spot was touched.

The accuser put the box down. Chagrined, he said, "Well, I guess I'm wrong. Must have been the light."

Doc straightened his vest, pulled on his string tie and said, "You just called me a cheat, which you'll have to answer for. You've bucked the tiger. Noon tomorrow show up at the ballfield on Goodwin Street. You and I are going to have us a duello."

"What's that?" Dilley asked.

"That's Italian for a duel, hayseed. Be there. And bring your second and a doctor, if you can find one. The choice of weapons is going to be a little different. No swords, no pistols, just something my carpenter friend has worked up. You'll find out when you get there. We call it Preskitt Duello Rules."

"Wait a minute. I didn't do anything. I just asked...."

"Too bad. You just besmirched my good name. See you at the ballfield. Noon tomorrow. Don't be late, or else."

That ended the game and everyone at the table scattered out the door or over to the bar where they started talking about the duel; taking bets on the outcome.

The next morning, the principals walked up Goodwin Street and through the gate to the ballfield. They stared at a loud, belching machine that was hissing and letting off steam and sooty smoke from its stack as a fireman shoved lengths of wood into its maw and adjusted the gauges.

Two long rubber hoses came out of its side with gun-like implements at the end of each. The devices were identical and each looked like a handgun with a large cylinder up by the front end. A cloud of steam was coming from the barrels of both. Closer inspection showed the cylinders in the guns held a clip of twelve objects. The objects were three-inch nails used in barn building.

The steam-driven nail gun inventor, Elmer Hawkins, was a

carpenter and tinkerer by inclination. He'd made his fortune in the gold fields of California. He put together his device after noting the flood of immigrants coming west and that there wasn't enough housing for them. Elmer needed a way to build buildings and barns faster. Not everyone was a builder so the newcomers wound up living in tents waiting for a few good carpenters to build them a house for the family and a barn and outbuildings for the livestock.

He came up with his steam-driven nail gun with a shuttle spindle and an automatic stop system. This device moved the construction process along faster than driving nails by hand. It could spit out one nail at a time with a trigger pull and could put a board in place in seconds. A replacement nail cylinder clip could be inserted as the first was exhausted.

Elmer was a card player and a friend of Doc's, so the two of them cooked up the weapon of choice for Doc's duello—Elmer's steam-gun nailer.

Towards eleven o'clock the next day, crowds started coming to the ballfield. Someone was going to get shot. They showed up just like they did at the public hangings. They had to see the event so they could say they were there. Many of them had money on the line. The odds were five to one in Doc's favor.

Dilley Browne knew this duello was not a good idea, but there didn't seem to be any good way to get out of it. At the ballfield, he brought his five brothers as seconds, thirds, fourths, fifth and sixths, but he couldn't find a doctor to stand by in case he got wounded.

At eleven fifty-five, Doc's second, Harry Cowlitz, went to the center of the ballfield and dropped a white handkerchief placing a stone on it so it wouldn't blow away. Then, he told the principals to take their positions. Harry went to the steam machine and brought the steam-guns out and handed one to Dilley and one to Doc. Moving to the side out of the line of fire, he explained how the steam-gun worked. Then he reviewed the Preskitt duello rules to one and all.

"Starting at the dropped cloth, back to back, you will each pace

ten steps away from each other on my count. When I say *ten*, you'll take another step, turn and fire at will. Whoever draws first blood, satisfaction will be called and you will shake hands and that will be the end of it. Agreed?" Harry yelled out.

The two parties nodded in unison.

On the count of ten, both stepped out and whirled. Dilley shot first, missing. Doc took only a second, aimed the steam-gun and pulled the trigger a dozen times. Twelve nails flew through the air and whanged into Dilley's right leg. Dilley dropped his gun, started howling and hopped over to his brothers.

"Kill that son of a bitch, boys. Look what he did to me!" Dilley shouted.

"Hold it!" Harry, Doc's second, yelled. He was holding a shotgun on the Browne brothers. "One move and you're going to be seeing Jesus."

"Yeah, Brownes, it's all fair and square," the crowd yelled as they stuffed their winnings into their pokes. The nails in Dilley's leg started to fall out. They'd only scratched him. At twenty paces between the duelers, the nails lost most of their impact, not to mention accuracy, and only stung a little bit.

Meanwhile, Doc walked over to Dilley, shook his hand and said, "You're a lucky cowhand Dilley. Usually, it's morticians you'll see next after my gun slinging. Today was just a bit of fun. Next time you're in a card game, watch your mouth. Now, you and your brothers go on home."

HOLY WATER

WE NEED WATER; we are water, 60 percent, plus or minus. Water is unusual compared to other fluids. It's the universal solvent because more substances dissolve in water than in any other chemical. Water is powerful and unstoppable; doesn't resist objects, flows around, over or under them. It is a highly concentrated force as well as an extremely soft one. Water will lift houses from their foundations, tear down mountains or bathe a child. Water provides inspiration for clarity—of mind, purpose and to cleanse.

I got involved in a water project after reading Dr. Roentgen's amazing research paper: *Ueber eine neue Art von Strahlen* (*On a New Kind of Rays*), published in the December issue of the 1895 German Chemical Society's Journal *Angewande Chemie*. I immediately wrote and asked to join him with one of my interfaces for the cathode ray tube that I knew he was experimenting with. A few weeks later, a neatly scribed letter arrived in the mail inviting me to collaborate in several experiments. I joyfully accepted.

When I arrived at his university laboratory in Munich, Dr. Roentgen greeted me. He stood five-foot-ten, wearing a dark suit with a gold watch fob peeking out of a vest pocket. His full mustache, black beard, and thick sideburns almost hid his face and neck. When he spoke, it reminded me of a crow flapping his wings, all that facial hair became animated and alive. A loose tie decorated his white shirt that was dappled with incongruous spots, probably from spattered chemicals. He was an imposing man, and he welcomed me with an enthusiastic "*Guten Morgen*" and a strong handshake, bustling me into his lab to show me all his projects. I immediately felt we were going to have a good working relationship.

Without wasting time, he mentioned his current experiment based on a suggestion that praying over dirty water could cleanse it. The idea came from several sources. For instance, the Bible mentions water over 700 times in the context of purification and cleansing. Water also has a central place in the practice and beliefs of most religions for two reasons: it cleanses, and it is the building block of life. By clean water, Dr. Roentgen explained that he meant potable water or improved drinking water that is safe to drink or use for food preparation, without the risk of health problems.

Thus, we set out to see if praying over dirty water would cleanse it using scientific methods to verify whether it worked and to what degree.

This idea was sparked by a visit from Japanese scientist and homeopathic physician, Dr. Haruko Amagawa. He read one of Roentgen's articles and was excited about it. He wrote Roentgen about a theory of cleansing water by praying over it. Dr. Amagawa said he got the idea from a Shinto priest whom he had met while visiting the Meiji Jingu shrine in the Shibuya Temple in Tokyo. The priest was enthusiastic about this concept and said he'd seen it work over and over. However, there was no proof that it worked except his say-so. We had heard elsewhere that this concept was pure bunkum postulated by charlatans. A truly scientific study was needed and we were going to test the theory. By thoroughly investigating, we were going to find out with a certainty.

I sent water samples to various religious groups: Buddhists, Islamic Shiites, Hindus, and Lutherans, who all agreed to cooperate in this experiment. Identical water samples were delivered in opaque brown glass bottles to the selected religious denominations.

We told each religious group the quality of the water was foul,

or non-potable. The samples were intentionally polluted with soiling agents making the water dirty and harmful to drink. We told the Lutherans their sample too was foul, dirty water; however, in reality, it was clean, clear H2O to be used as a control. We instructed each group to pray over their water samples. The instructions included the following information: do not open or disturb the bottles once placed in position. Pray over the samples for one-half hour per day, at the same time of day for seven consecutive days. Say the conventional prayers of your religious group. On the eighth day, our courier would pick up the samples and bring them to Dr. Roentgen's laboratory at the Ludwig Maximillian University of Munich.

When they were returned, the water analysis project began immediately upon sample arrival at the lab. Dr. Roentgen set up his X-ray machine, and I connected it to my Interacting Chromatin Ray Filter (ICRF) that colorized the X-rays when projected onto Dr. Roentgen's barium platinocyanide base. Color images were formed on a three-layer gelatin colloid film from the CRT projection. These were used for the analysis along with a chromaticity chart developed by a Herr Vogel.

After the water samples were X-rayed, the images would have a chromatic spectrum of colors instead of black and white renderings. It was easier to interpret color instead of the typical gray scale with a black to white continuum.

Dr. Roentgen discovered that the theory of water is all wrong. Using his X-ray machine and tuning the rays to a specific range of energies, he previously revealed the arrangements of water molecules. He found out the composition of water is made up of two structures. One is tetrahedral or "ice-like" and the second, a more loosely arranged formation. These structures explain why water behaves in such unusual ways.

Before beginning our experiment, we established that dirty water, when color X-rayed, looks red, or some hue of red, depending on the degree of its pollution. Clean water when X-rayed, takes a hue of green, sometimes into the violet spectrum. If praying over water cleans it, this has implications for millions of people. Many drink foul water every day. Clean water could result in no more typhoid, no more cholera, no more giardiasis, hepatitis, dysentery, amebiasis nor myriads of other waterborne diseases.

When the samples were returned from the prayer groups, we found the colorized X-rayed water samples ranged across the electromagnetic spectrum from red (still dirty) to green (clean). Some samples were even a little into the violet (even cleaner).

The Lutherans, our control group's water, was still clear or displayed green, so praying had no effect on their sample. The Buddhists' water came back a pinkish red; the Shiites' sample was burnt Siena or orange and the Hindus' a Kelly green—the purest of the lot. We had to conclude the Buddhists didn't pray very hard; the Shiites did a little better. The Hindus did the best and created the cleanest water.

To see if the different groups believed in our theory, we asked each group to drink the water sample they'd prayed over without letting them know the results. The Buddhists declined, the Shiites at least took a sip, and the Hindus drank the whole sample. A week later, the Shiites got a small fever that went away in a few days, while the Hindus stayed healthy. Interestingly enough, all the Lutherans got violently sick after drinking their clean water sample, but all recovered. Dr. Roentgen said he'd have to tell his psychiatrist friend Dr. Ludwig Meyer about this. He thought it must have been a psychosomatic reaction to telling them it was fouled or that they didn't have enough faith in their prayers.

We felt one problem with the study was the religious groups were told to pray for a defined time period and to do it consistently. Since this was not monitored, we couldn't say with any degree of certainty whether the prayer instructions were followed. A more rigorous study should be conducted to monitor the praying.

Empirical evidence indicates we are on the right track since more than one group attained pure water and others, almost pure water. We are fairly certain we are onto a way to confirm the theory that praying over water cleanses, but the methodology needs more work. It may depend on how consistently and how well the subjects pray. We will do another study to find out if different languages or prayer mantras are better than others in effecting water quality.

THE ORGANIST AND THE TENOR

"PLEASED TO MEET YOU," Lilly Norris said to Adrian Simms, the Music Master, who was interviewing her for an associate organist position at Westminster Abbey. Simms was a short, natty man with a professional air. Lilly noted on the abbey's music flyer that he had an MPhil. in Musicology from Cambridge.

"You have my resume, and of course, I know many of the classical hymns," she exclaimed.

"Let's try your hand at the Westminster Grand Organ, my dear. It has five manuals or keyboards, forty-five stops on either side for each of the pipes and a radiating concave peddle board. We have each applicant play a number of selections. Today, if you are ready, please play: *Amazing Grace*, then *How Great Thou Art*, and finally, *The Day Thou Gavest*."

Lilly took off her gloves, set them aside along with her hat and stepped up to the organ. She familiarized herself with the instrument for a few minutes. Dressed more for the inclement weather outside than for a recital, she limbered her fingers before stepping up to the keyboard.

She'd been making the rounds of churches for interviews and hadn't anticipated this opportunity. Nevertheless, she felt ready for it. She slid onto the padded organ bench, accustoming herself with the organ, its components and the feel of the instrument before beginning. Comfortable, she turned on the steam–driven bellows, checked the wind chest and pulled each of the 90 stops to listen. Lilly keyed her ear to the pitch and octave of the pipes and listened for their individual tonality. She worked her way down from the chorus ranks to the flutes, to the reeds, and finally to the strings. Satisfied with the instrument, she asked Mr. Simms, "G is the traditional key, will that be all right?"

"Perfect," he replied. "The steam power is up to pressure, so you may begin."

Lilly put her narrow shoes on the peddle board, opened the bellows, calibrated the keys, and began to play. Simms sang along as she played, "*Amazing grace how sweet the sound…*" All the way to the last line, "*thus when we first begun.*" Having finished all three hymns, she looked to the Music Master for his reaction.

"Wonderful, my dear, just wonderful," he announced. She'd not missed a note or sounded an off key. "I picked those hymns for you as they are Queen Victoria's favorites. You're the last of the applicants to audition for us. Now, I have to report to the committee. Should you be chosen, you will be notified by messenger. Good day."

A week later, the new associate organist at the abbey, Lilly, put all of her training and virtuosity into the keyboard and practiced with the choir. First, she met the choirmaster, Charles Barker, an older gentleman who worked with the choir to get them to sing as one. Lilly familiarized herself with the nuances of each of the singers by having them sing individually in their vocal range. Then, with the choirmaster, she worked with the choir to blend them to the key or scale needed for each piece played.

As the weeks went by, of all the singers in the choir, the tenor soloist, Paolo Raineri, became her favorite. A blind, wounded veteran and refugee from the first Italo-Ethiopian War of 1895, he delighted her with his exquisite high notes. When he sang, however, unusual things happened. The tinkle of glass hitting the floor of the nave was sometimes heard when Paolo hit his highest note. He could not only break crystal, but he blew out one of the small stained-glass windows depicting Jesus carrying the cross. He often hit resonance frequency

and shattered many an object with his powerful voice. The cathedral rang with the ecstasy of his high notes, each chasing the other from the chancel to the transept, to the nave, fading to the baptismal font in the narthex. The congregation wanted to applaud, but it was a church, so they just appreciated him.

Lilly became the favorite organist and the congregation swelled on the days she played. However, she sensed the organ was not quite right. It was a magnificent organ, but with all its pipes and stops, it didn't seem to perform at its best capacity of sound and sonorousness, no matter how well she played. She asked Mr. Simms to engage a tuner to monitor the organ's works for its inability to meet her expectations.

The tuner's analysis was the wind chest was just too anemic to get the maximum sound from the pipes. Simms engaged an engineer to add a steam-driven turbocharger to the bellows. When the new turbo was first installed the pressure blew up the largest pipe. Known as the "Voice of God," it was made of galvanized spotted-metal alloy and used only for the grandest music. Shrapnel of leaded–tin scattered down the empty nave, bouncing off the pews, inflicting little harm. Fortunately, it occurred in a practice session and neither the choir nor the congregation was there except Penny and Paolo.

When the big pipe was replaced, Simms said, "We need to calibrate the turbo, it has to be perfect for the Queen's up-coming celebration." The engineer returned and installed a variable pressure gauge that fixed the problem. With the organ recalibrated, the pipes' ranges increased. With Lilly's modulated playing, the artificial, augmented Aeolian wind pulsed the cathedral with an ethereal sound. It seemed as if the hand of God was playing the instrument now, instead of a mere mortal.

"Paolo, love, we need to test the organ with your voice. Join me. We can warm up on Bellini's, *I Puritani*, then move on to Puccini's *Che Gilida Manina* from *La Boheme*. We will test your voice and the notes and timbre of the mighty organ." With that, she turned the turbo to "full," and hoped Paolo would see her as more than a mere organist, but as a woman, a desirable woman who loved him.

Paolo, aware of her ardor for him could hear it in her voice when they spoke. But he couldn't see her and had never touched her. "Lilly, we will make music together. It will be wonderful to sing in my own language along with your beautiful notes."

Lilly pulled out all the stops, and began to play the score from Bellini's *I Puritani* as Paolo sang, *A te, o cara, amor talora, mi guido furtivo e in pianto; or mi guida a te d'accanto tra la gioia e l' esultar...* ("To you, oh dear one, love at times lead me furtively and in tears; now it guides me to your side in joy and exultation.") When it ended, Paolo walked over and gave Lilly a hug. Then, she played Puccini's famous aria from La Boheme, *Che gilida manina, se la lasci riscaldar...* ("What a frozen little hand, let me warm it.")

As the music rose to the rafters, the cathedral seemed to be enveloped in waves of sound. Paolo hit ascending notes and the tinkle of glass could be heard. As Lilly played, the pipes roared with the melody. She felt wrapped in love, a duet of shimmering sound. At the highest pitch, the turbo whirred, and the pipes pulsated. Lilly played with all her heart and Paolo hit his highest note. Windows shattered and the pipes exploded, scattering glass and metallic fragments in a storm of death. The cathedral pulsated, shaking as cold air flew through empty stained-glass portals.

The next day, *The Daily Telegraph* reported that an evil wind must have taken hold of the organ that killed two young promising musicians.

PACIFIC LOW

ON SUNDAY, OCTOBER 29,1865, El Nino, acted up. The monsoon season brought in a low-pressure system, a Pacific cyclonic storm. It hit the Hawaiian Islands, especially Maui. Thunder, lightning, and hail knocked down trees, saturating everything and everybody in sight. The wind ruffled the trees, blowing leaves and flowers around like asteroids showering the heavens. The odor of frangipani, candlenut, acacia, jacaranda, hibiscus, ohia lehua, and other trees perfumed the air like a giant spritzer loosened to smother the island in scent. Ice pellets bounced off metal roofs with a continuous riff, like mad steel drums playing an unknown melody.

Pele, the Hawaiian goddess of lightning, wind, volcanoes, and dance rampaged that night. Hawaiians think of Pele as their special protector and know she can be arbitrary and capricious. Many people say they have seen her, usually in a long, flowing red muumuu accompanied by a small white dog of no known breed. She threw a tantrum that night.

Meanwhile, Eunice Obrigado lay in her bedroom in Lahaina waiting to give birth. A midwife monitored her labor.

"Alani, he's coming. Finally, oh, to have this over with. My baby, my sweet little child," Eunice panted between contractions.

Just as the baby crowned, a microburst hit the island of Maui, her house, and the neighbor's homes. Part of the roof over the kitchen blew off when the downdraft struck.

The father, Enrico, a *luna* or manager at the local Hohanapata sugar mill plantation, rode home in the storm when informed his wife was about to give birth. When he arrived, he rejoiced at the new arrival, then went to work fixing the roof to keep out the rain.

In the calm of the following day, Eunice remembering her traumatic delivery and the devastation of the storm, said, "Let's call him 'Boomba.'" In respect for the storm, she considered it an auspicious moment, and both she and her husband confirmed his nickname: "Boomba," for the violent downdraft that pelted the island as he entered the world.

Before the birth, Enrico and Eunice Obrigado had sat at the kitchen table debating a name for the baby.

"What are we going to call our first born?" Enrico asked.

"Let explore the relatives Christian names. *vovo*, (grandmother) thinks it's a boy so we can concentrate there," responded Eunice.

Enrico wanted to name him Tomaz, after his father, a noted musician, and fisherman from Madeira, Portugal. Eunice had other ideas and wanted to name him Miguel, after her home island, San Miguel in the Azores, another Portuguese island in the Atlantic Ocean.

Both parents had individually and separately responded to advertisements for free passage to Hawaii under a labor contract with the Hawaiian government to work on a sugarcane plantation. The deal included an acre of land, a house, and improved working conditions. Enrico and Eunice found each other in the cane fields and married. As Portuguese nationals, they received favored status compared to the Japanese, Filipinos, and Chinese workers. They also had better jobs like managers or *lunas* and acted as intermediaries between the Asians and the owners. Still, their status remained below that of the *haole* white owners.

Weeks before the birth, Eunice's *vovo*, Agueda, who lived with them, had taken Eunice's wedding ring and tied a foot-long string on it. She had her granddaughter lie down on the bed and held the thread over her distended belly. If the ring circled, it was a boy, if the ring swung side to side, a girl. It went in circles. With that information, the parents agreed to the sex of the child, and they prepared to give him a unique identity before he showed up. Perusing baby-naming books, they exhausted the lists. Dredging up all the names of their respective relatives, they also looked for names in the local newspapers and rejected them. They compromised on the Christian names of Portuguese heroes and leaders as their choice for the baby's name: Antonio Rodriguez Ronaldo Tomaz Miguel Pedro Obrigado.

As they volleyed speculative names for the child, the moon shone in full state, a *Hoku* moon, known as the spirit walkers moon according to Hawaiian meteorology and myth. Eunice's Zodiac charts told her their son would be a Scorpio if he arrived between October 23rd and November 21st. She believed he would emulate the forecasts for his sign. He would have patience and charm, would be clear thinking and willful. A Scorpio could accomplish what his head and heart wanted most. Among other traits, he would be brave, passionate, stubborn, an honest friend, trusting, jealous, secretive, and violent.

As he grew, Boomba seldom responded to any of the formal names bestowed upon him. If you wanted his attention, you called him Boomba. He grew into a handsome young man with black, curly hair and an engaging smile that delighted his mother and the girls he met. At five foot ten, slender, deeply tanned, and athletic, he loved to dance, swim, and surfboard.

Seventeen years after his birth, in October of 1882, Boomba graduated from Lahainaluna Seminary, a high school, ready for the world of work. With few prospects other than farm labor, he turned to his father for employment on the plantation. Enrico, who had risen to foreman or *luna* in charge of personnel and placement for the plantation, knew the best job for his son would be to learn as many aspects of raising and processing sugarcane from the ground on up.

Boomba hired as a hoe man to weed the cane joined the *kelai* or gangs of men, women, and children. Doing this he would understand how important it was to keep the weeds down and rid the vermin and dried leaves from the cane. He'd done this many times before as a child during summer vacations with other children.

Hoeing cane fields subjected the workers to hard labor with constant exposure to the elements. As good as the weather was, everyone still had to deal with the sun, rain, wind, soil dust, soot from burned sugarcane leaves, bugs, venomous animals, and the sharp edges of the cane leaf. Pay for the individuals in the hoe gangs depended on the number of lines hoed. Each line was three feet wide and sixty feet long. A worker received one half-cent to twelve cents per line, depending on the number of weeds. For an eight-hour day of steady, hard work, even the best hoers seldom made more than a dollar.

Keeping the weeds down and preparing the ground for the next ratoon necessitated this hand labor. Sugarcane, like rice and bananas, grows from the stubble of the previous crop, or ratoon, already harvested. The hoers didn't just weed the crop; they also removed silt and debris from the irrigation and drainage ditches to keep them open. All the local plantations shared irrigation water for their fields from a lake in the mountains by way of a long water ditch.

Boomba soon made friends with the field workers. They spoke different languages, but Hawaiian pidgin was their universal tongue. Foreign laborers were brought in to supplement the lack of Hawaiians available to work this labor intensive crop. The plantation's workers were Japanese, Chinese, Korean, Filipino, Puerto Rican, German, Portuguese, and Hawaiians. Without a common language, pidgin was the *lingua franca*. Boomba exceeded in both pidgin and as a *hoehana* or hoe man. Recognized for his skills, he next became a cane chopper.

After work, he'd spend time with the Hawaiians to surf and dance at their hangouts. He felt most comfortable with them, loved to compete in surfing contests, going to their dances, and learning their language, but knew he'd never be fully accepted. As the son of a *luna* and soon to become one, he'd always be *Dat Pawdagee haole* (the Portuguese white boy), no matter how much he imitated them.

Boomba loved to create new things. He had a deep curiosity

about what mattered to him. But he passionately loved to dance, any dance, especially, new ones coming from the mainland plus traditional Hawaiian ones. He liked to hang out with the Hawaiians at their Friday night dances at the plantation clubhouse. He also searched for new dances and learned their associated dance steps. He found sheet music and steps for the Cakewalk, the Gallup, the Mazurka, the Polka, and other new and popular music on the mainland. He wrote to music publishers for sheet music and dance steps. He took the music sheet to his Hawaiian buddies in the band and had them orchestrated to the traditional Hawaiian musical instruments ukulele, guitar, gourds (*ipu*), flute (*hano*), sticks (*pu'ili*) and drum (*punio*).

The cane, scorched from burning, got rid of twenty-five percent of the dried leafy trash. The burning didn't hurt the sugar content in the cane, just left sooty stalks to be cut. Twelve hour days chopping cane in over ninety plus degree heat left Boomba and the field hands exhausted. But, the stalks had to be gathered and bundled for loading. The 80 to 100 pound bundles then had to be piled onto a mule train. At the end of the work day, after sweating from the heat, cutting, carrying, and stowing the cane on the mill transport trains, they usually headed for the beach.

After a season of this work, Boomba petitioned his father for a job in the mill machine shop. He explained a few ideas he had for improvements.

Enrico got Boomba a job as an apprentice welder—welding any tools or machinery on the plantation that broke. Plenty of work presented itself since carts, ladles, rollers, hoes, and other hard–used tools and machinery broke and often needed repair. Repairing broken machinery during the harvest season became especially critical when the plantation mill worked 24 hour days, seven days a week until harvest and processing finished. Any tool or machinery could break down while the equipment worked harvesting, milling, boiling, and centrifuging cane juice.

Learning the welding trade and working on the plantation

machinery, Boomba became the man to go to. As one of the lunas said of him, "Dat Boomba boy he plenny *akamai* (smart)."

Mill machinery broke down with regularity. At times the rollers in the press house would jump out of line when forcing too much cane through them. It would jam and stop the drive machinery. This malfunction would, in turn, seize up the drive gears and break gear teeth, which would then bind up the machinery.

"Boomba, what's with the steam boiler?" Fumihiro, the Japanese boilerman asked. "It's offline. We need to get it going. Harvest starts in a few weeks."

"I know. It's only been down for a few hours," Boomba replied. "We have to drain the boiler to change the fire tube. One either corroded or overheated and burst and is leaking. After I drain the boiler and replace the tube, we can get it back online. It'll take a week or more, though. I have to get replacement tubes shipped in from Oahu since none are stockpiled on site."

"How long will that take?" Fumihiro asked.

"At least two weeks. No way to telegraph for replacements. I'll have to send the order with the inter-island steamer when it arrives tomorrow in Lahaina. We hope they have the right tubes in stock at the warehouse in Honolulu."

Supply problems were a common event. If something broke at a critical moment or just before, panic would set in for whoever needed it or worked with the equipment. Being on an island in the middle of the Pacific Ocean didn't help the supply chain for new or replacement parts.

Improving things fired Boomba's interest. One of his innovations became a self-propelled, automatic cane cutter. He invented a small steam traction engine with a chain belt drive for the rear axle with a leather belt drive off of a flywheel for his cane cutter. The cutter made out of four machete blades welded 90 degrees apart horizontally from each other connected to a rotating wheel. In action, this cutter could be lowered to cut sugarcane stalks at their base, then raised for transport.

The plantation overseer, Charles Dwyer, did not approve of Boomba's inventions. He told Boomba to quit working on them since it took time away from plant operations. The overseer, a retired sea captain from Nantucket, did not want any uppity workers trying new things or doing anything not approved by him.

Boomba initially got the idea for his machines from the *Progressive Farmer* magazine to which he subscribed. Steam tractors were new and gaining popularity, and he studied their design. With scrap steel from the plantation junkyard, he welded together a boiler, set it on top of a four-wheel drive unit with a crude steering wheel. Secretly he continued his project against Dwyer's objection. Late at night when everyone had gone home, he worked hours into the night in his welding shop to fabricate it with no one around. In front of his cutter, he jury-rigged his dangerous rotating machete chopper wheel. His first unit could only cut a single row of sugarcane at a time. With trial and error, he improved his machine. Finally assembled, he took it to a remote field on a moonlit night and chopped a row of cane to prove it worked.

A lot of his first welds didn't work as well as they should have. Machetes flew off the spinning cutter wheel after only a few cane chops which would have endangered anyone nearby. At ten o'clock at night, with no one present, it didn't matter. At that time of night, families and staff retired to be ready for the next morning's 4:00 a.m. wake up for the work day. People who rose early worked ten-hour days, six days a week could be found in bed early.

The problems Boomba encountered included: a drive belt kept slipping; the steel traction wheels spun losing grip when they hit a wet or muddy patch, and the firebox proved to be too small to keep a good head of steam on the drive unit. After every fix, the traction engine improved. Dwyer, sensing something was still going on in the weld shop asked one of the staff to report to him what Boomba was up to. He knew machines were an opportunity to speed up production, but wasn't sure now was the time for them.

When the harvest ended, Boomba was still working on his machine into the night, and figured his single-row cutter could do the same work as five field hands. But, this machine couldn't do the manual grunt work of loading the cut stalks onto the mill train afterward, as a cane cutter would.

Hawaiian workers found cut cane in a far corner of the plantation. The wobbly ten to twelve-foot high cane stalks hadn't lodged or been blown down. Rather, the foot of the stalks bore neat cuts. Wheel marks in the ground indicated mechanized cutting. Apprehensive and wondering how this occurred, the workers decided to keep track of the different cane groves on the 2,000-acre plantation not yet scheduled for harvesting. Anything disturbing to the existing work methods could create panic if it affected their livelihood. Curious about this, the workers decided to tell the boss man, Dwyer.

Dwyer found out about Boomba's continuing nightly machinations to improve harvesting with his new-fangled machine. Several of the Asian cutters also told him about the mysteriously cut cane found in a remote field. They were concerned since once the cane is cut, the brix, or sugar, starts to evaporate, so it was being wasted just lying in the field. Dwyer confronted Boomba about his invention and demanded to know why he continued to work on it when he'd been told to stop; plus, chopping cane without permission and just leaving it to lie in the field couldn't be tolerated.

Boomba, not exactly contrite, launched into a desperate argument that tractors like his were on their way to agriculture and would soon be ubiquitous. Then, he pointed out how they might easily improve production by cutting cane faster than by hand, and be able to make more sugar with fewer employees. Alternately, they could expand acreage with more fields to increase their sugar output with the same number of employees.

Dwyer listened then said, "I want to see this. We'll set up a trial. If your machine is working tomorrow, I'll have a cane cutter down at field number P-19 at six o'clock in the morning. You be there with your chopper. You'll each have a sixty-foot standard row to cut. I'm timing the event, Boomba. We will see if you are still going to be working in the weld shop or go back to the *kelai* gangs. I'll have a crew pick up the cane afterward."

Fortunately for Boomba, his machine beat the field hand by a huge margin and Dwyer was finally convinced that mechanization beat the old ways of farming.

Over the years, the Hawaiians had seen a young lady strolling in a red muumuu around the plantation followed by her little white dog. She came to their dances on several weekends and danced with the most handsome men. No one knew her, and most thought she was a friend of someone else at the dance. Someone started a rumor that Pele had come to their dance. She was known to love to dance and especially, the hula. When Hiapo Makani, a 6' 4" *kanaka* cane cutter and surfer asked by a friend who he'd danced with, said, "I don't know bradda, but she sure knew how to swing dem hips."

"Well, you going to see her again? She your *Nui Ku'uipo* (big sweetheart)?"

"I don't think so. She just grabbed another bradda after we danced and twirled away. She fabulous and loved the rhythm. She didn't talk, just got into the moves. Nobody was going to turn that *wahine* down. Then she flitted away. Her little dog sat on the side watching her."

Boomba danced with the lady, too. He'd danced with her before at other dances. He liked her. She was *ho onani* (beautiful). Of course, the muumuu didn't do anything for her figure, but she certainly had the moves to the music. She said her name was Pepi, or that's what he heard over the music. She asked him what he'd like to do after the dance. Not used to such a forward suggestion, his only reply was, "How about a coke and a *malasada* at the cantina?" This was not what she had in mind. She rephrased it, "Wen go foa da beach wid me. Go ho' oipoipo. Wot?

Embarrassed, he turned her down saying, "I've welding to do back at the shop. Maybe another night." Pepi had made this suggestion before at another dance, and he'd turned her down then too with a lame excuse. Boomba seemed to be more interested in the dancing than in the girls he danced with. The girls though, were interested in him for all his detachment.

Annoyed, she gave him a dirty look and said, "We *pau* (finished, done)" and swung off to dance with another fellow.

After his success with his first cane cutter machine, Boomba built a triple-row traction engine cutter and made plans for more machines. When the field workers heard about this and saw the prototype harvester being built in the weld shop, they became worried. If the cane was going to be cut by machines, they were going to be out of work.

The Hawaiians felt threatened and prayed to their protector, Pele, who lived in Mauna Loa on the Big Island but controlled the island volcanoes. Although the old customs and native religion were banished by the missionaries in the early 1800s, some Hawaiians, now ostensibly Christian, kept to the old ways. The Cult of Pele still lived. She was the Hawaiian people's protector, though at times, a jealous, capricious and very arbitrary deity. Recognizing this, the Hawaiians out of respect for her, fearfully referred to her as "Madame Pele."

Dwyer, observing the machine improvements Boomba made, became persuaded the plantation needed these innovations. So convinced of the machine's value to increase production, he ordered two, new tractors currently coming on the market and that could be used on the plantation.

The Hawaiian cane cutters, now thoroughly frightened for their jobs, called on Pele, *Ka Wahine ʻai honaua* (the earth-eating woman) to keep their jobs. They prayed to her that these new machines threatened their livelihood. If these chattering, smoky new steam clankers took over the cane cutting and other jobs, they were back to growing taro and fishing for a living. They entreated her to banish them so they would not be pushed off the plantation by these new noisy devils.

Boomba, totally engrossed in his new inventions was unaware of the implications that his machines would have on the local culture and economy. Charging ahead, his next innovation turned into a steam-driven road locomotive to replace the cane hauling mule trains. Again, unaware of the misgivings of the Hawaiian laborers and their employment concerns, Boomba merrily welded from day into the late hours of the night. At the mill site, he built a roundtable for the engines so the locomotives could easily be turned around to return to the fields.

The road locomotive had steel wheels to meet the narrow gauge track, and additional track spurs found their way to the remotest fields of the plantation. These innovations enabled the harvest to be transported to the mill in a very quick way. The faster, the better because, the longer it took to get the cut cane in, the more moisture and sugar content would be lost to evaporation.

Six months later, the new tractors arrived from Iowa. On docking day, the steamer arrived on schedule with passengers, freight, and mail, including two shiny new Waterloo Gasoline Traction Engine Company tractors, painted pine green.

Word spread that all the Hawaiians should come to a community dance downtown in Lahaina. They were to bring everyone; their children, their parents, their grandparents, everyone in their family to the dance. No one was to be left behind on the plantation. No one knew who ordered them to comply. No matter, it was a party.

As the steamer pulled in, a tropical cyclone sweeping west, struck the island with lightning, thunder, and rain. Pele had a mad-on. She was peeved, pissed, perturbed and resentful that a little *Pawdegee haole* turned her down. When she wanted *hoaloha* and *kaunu*, she expected it. She, not *Queen Lilioukalani* ruled Hawaii, and would demonstrate it.

Back at the Hohanapata Plantation, fissures opened along the property lines. *Ah-ah* lava, gas, and molten rock oozed from the ground like hot jello, slowly moving across the land paving over everything in its path. The plantation workers still at home rushed to save themselves when they heard the earth crack and saw the bubbling stream of red

death inching towards them.

Pele unleashed hot lava on the Hohanapata plantation. She directed the Wailuku volcano to the west to create dikes and fissures in the earth as pathways to scold the offending *haole* and his plantation. It was as though a guided hand drew a line to the multi-acre plantation and cleaved open cavities in the earth along its boundaries.

At the quay-side, Dwyer gave Boomba the key to a new tractor that was off-loaded at the Lahaina seaport. Boomba held the key aloft so all could see, and a thin bolt of lightning struck the key and the hand that held it.

It was October 29, 1895, his 30th birthday, his last birthday ever. With luck, perseverance, and stubbornness, Boomba had accomplished what his heart desired and met much of his mother's forecast for his Scorpio sign.

In town, the Hawaiians danced in the rain, unaware of their rescue from the lava enveloping their homes and workplace. A woman dressed in a colorful muumuu was in the middle of the dance floor having picked out a good looking guy to dance with and enthralled him with her sinuous moves. In the shadow of the crowd, a little white dog looked on.

In the days following when the sky cleared, and the rough weather moved on, Dwyer surveyed the plantation as best he could. He wanted to see what was left. The view was a smoking desert of *ah-ah* lava, with the plantation under twelve to fifteen feet of cooling fire rock. Smoke from the burning buildings flavored the air with soot and burning cane leaves. The fried sugarcane aromatized the wind like burnt caramel with bitter hints of blackstrap molasses. Occasional fiery eruptions spewed from the lava blanket as oil and other combustibles caught fire under the mill works, the housing, and the machines. The Hohanapata Plantation sizzled.

THE SÉANCE

EVERY MONTH the Trafalgars invited guests up from London for their séances. These were attempts to make contact with the dead through the use of a medium. Famous clairvoyants were engaged for these presentations. On more than one of these occasions, guests complained about hearing thumping and shrieking sounds above their bedroom ceiling, as though someone was having a party.

The Trafalgars, aware the commotion occurred at different times, saw no pattern. Concerned, they attributed the noise to the plumbing and called in the village plumbers for a solution. The tradesmen declared the waterworks sound. Whatever the cause, the above-stairs merry-making and carrying-on past retiring time continued sporadically. With no solution found, they simply hoped the problem would go away.

At breakfast, Lady Asquint, a guest, bemoaned, "Gloria, I don't know who or what is up in your attic, but they certainly don't abide decent hours. Bertie and I were kept awake forever."

"Oh, Jane, I'm so sorry," replied Lady Gloria Trafalgar, "We've had this complaint before, but found no solution. Every time we check the attic, it's quiet. I can't imagine why it would be so noisy or where it would come from. It's just filled with all the souvenirs from our postings to the colonies and some spare furniture. We sleep in a different part of the house and never hear it, so are not bothered. No one has ever said the house was haunted."

When more than one set of guests had complained, Lady Gloria became so concerned, she knew she had to do something or their friends would quit coming to the country. She penned a note to Miss Fay Falconer, a noted exorcist and ghost hunter. In her message she explained her problem and why she needed help immediately.

"Carlyle, take the coach and deliver this message, please. Ask Miss Fay Falconer to come at once. I'm desperate and I believe she is the only one who can help us. Tell her to bring her ghost busting kit and evening clothes. She can join us for dinner and the séance after she sets up her equipment to catch whatever is making the racket in the attic."

In London, Miss Falconer scanned the note Carlyle delivered. Excited to go to the country and to use her skills, Fay packed an overnight valise, her most fashionable evening dress, and hurried down the staircase. She had Carlyle load her ghost-busting equipment from the hallway storeroom onto the coach.

Fay arrived to find the house full of guests. When all introductions were made and the situation explained to the guests, she set to work. The visitors watched her supervise the household staff in bringing box after box into the foyer.

She took Lady and Lord Trafalgar aside and explained, "Thank you for bringing me here. I'm sure I can rid your attic of the noise makers. I've done this many times and had a very good success rate. But, please keep the guests away, it could be dangerous."

Picking up a large wooden spool, a box, and set of wires with bent handles from her kit and, directed by staff, she climbed to the attic door. Opening the door cautiously, she warned the butler, "Stand back, there may be evil doings within."

Windows at either end of the garret attic illuminated a dusty area. She could discern stacks of wooden crates, boxes and unused furniture stored around the eaves. As she walked in and pulled off dust covers, she noted the shelves were loaded with carvings, swords, spears, military shakos, a stuffed crocodile, a boar's head, and racks of guns. There was also a large box containing a jumble of puppets. Miss

Falconer rummaged through them, pulling them out of the box and admiring them one by one. A fierce looking Indian warrior puppet had a smug face and a large sword clutched in its hand. The sword looked like it had a swath of blood on it, or maybe it was only dull red paint. It was hard to tell in the dim light. Some of the puppets had chips of wood hacked out of their sides and looked broken. A female puppet appeared untouched and displayed a moon symbol on its side. It was beautifully carved and adorned with a dress of gold threads and a gauzy silk blouse. The puppet also had a veil and jewelry dangled from her neck and wrist; small letters on the side of the puppet said: *Avantika*, while a scalloped gold chain encircled her waist.

Using her dowsing rods, Fay scanned the room for signs of anything that could have caused the ruckus. Investigating every corner of the attic, all seemed normal. No twitch or vibration from the rods alerted her sensitive hands. No hint, clue, or feeling of any kind of presence alerted her canny senses. Next, she beckoned Jones, the butler, to bring up her ghost hunting materials from the boxes downstairs.

First, she set up her ambient thermometer to measure any unusual heat source. Then she installed several aural amplifier cones and asked Jones to attach them to the brass voice pipe that connected to the kitchen where the servants congregated. The butler helped her unpack her motion detector kit with its battery powered component and set it up. She connected her teslameter to the battery as well. When the bell rang, she would be alerted to any form of magnetism. Lastly, Fay unspooled thin, strong black thread from her tool kit, arranged trip-wires throughout the attic a foot above the floor, and connected them to a horn. Any disturbance of the threads would set off this electrical klaxon with decibel levels as high as a shriek and loud enough to be heard throughout the manor. It, too, was connected to the second amplifier cone and the speaking tube.

Back in the drawing room, Miss Falconer found Lady Trafalgar and made a request, "Would you please assign your staff to round-the-clock listening in the kitchen. It may be the only way we can catch whoever it is in the attic." The household staff was appointed to shifts. A few were unhappy because they had to be up all hours, plus do their usual chores.

Miss Falconer, shown to her room to change into her evening clothes, later joined the Trafalgars and their guests for dinner. Afterwards, they planned to try to contact Harold's deceased Uncle Edgar, who'd been garroted by a Hindu fanatic after serving roast beef to his Indian officers. Edgar had been a colonel in the British East India Company's Army stationed in Bombay, and a noted collector of folk-art which Lord Harold inherited.

After a sumptuous dinner, the Trafalgars and their guests retired to the parlor for the evening's entertainment. Madame Sztama, a popular clairvoyant, asked everyone at the table to stand up and join hands. She called for Uncle Edgar to join them and give a sign that he appeared, while everyone waited expectantly. At first, there was no sound in the darkened room. Then, there came a small, very faint thumping, almost a Morse Code, and the table began to rise and a ghostly voice said, "Nephew Harold, how good of you to call me. I understand you have a problem."

Lady Gloria responded, "Oh, Edgar, we need your assistance. The manor is haunted and we don't know what to do."

"It's simple my dear," said the ghostly voice haltingly, "Have your exorcist hang a sheet by the attic window. She should take the puppets out of the box and position them behind it. Then, have watchers hidden in the attic, ready to pounce. Should the puppets come alive and start dancing and carousing or attacking one another, jump in and capture the aggressor."

The voice started to trail off. "I have to go; the air is killing me." The table thumped to the floor and the candle lights mysteriously blinked and went out. Uncle Edgar was gone.

Miss Falconer told the Trafalgars she would follow Uncle Edgar's suggestion. She returned to the attic, set up the sheet and laid out the puppets. Looking through the dusty books in the attic, she found a

volume inscribed by Uncle Edgar. It was a collection of East Indies' folk tales and traditional *wayang* (puppetry) stories. She found a chair in a dark corner, reading the puppet stories while waiting in the dim light.

When the full moon came out that night, it rose slowly on the horizon and began to illuminate the murky attic. As it rose and shone through the windows, the puppets began to stand up without the help of a puppeteer. Their control sticks hung uselessly on their strings, as they began to assemble behind the sheet and started dancing. To no music but their own, they deftly stepped to a hidden rhythm. Slow at first, then faster and faster, they made a huge racket as they pounded together on the floor. The moon shone on them and powered their steps. They were as wild as drunken Sufi dervishes in their mad whirling, twisting, spinning chaotic dance. As they swirled and whirligiged, they knocked over boxes, sent dusty books flying and made a madhouse racket that reverberated through the attic. It must have sounded like the banshees of hell to the floor below.

Silhouetted against the sheet, they danced and played. Abruptly the sword-wielding puppet, the fierce looking one with *Ramayan* inscribed on its side, raised his sword against one of the dancing puppets who tried to cut in on him and *Avantika* while they were dancing. Miss Falconer lunged at him, putting him in an arm lock, so he didn't get to use it. All the other puppets stopped, jumped into their box, and went silent. She brought the fierce puppet downstairs and showed the Trafalgars and the guests. It was only a wooden figure with puppeteer's sticks that control the head, arms, and legs.

"It's the moon madness that makes them dance," she said. "It's strongest when there is a full moon like there is tonight. This evil puppet, *Ramayan*, has injured or destroyed other puppets who wooed *Avantika*, the Queen of the Moon. He was jealous and wanted her for himself." Miss Falconer went on to suggest, "Seal up the windows or seal the box of puppets, then you'll have no more troubles in the attic. Keep them in the dark."

Miss Falconer saved the puppet *Avantika* from *Ramayan*. Tranquil nights followed. No more guests were disturbed and Lady Gloria sighed a breath of relief that the mad dancing and attic noise was over and their guests would no longer be disturbed.

Lord Harold bound up the puppet *Ramayan* with rope and stored him in the stable. On the next full moon, the Trafalgars held a bonfire attended by a number of guests who were antique dealers. Lord Harold held an impromptu auction. High bidder took *Ramayan*. Fortunately for the puppet, an agent for Taylor's Auction house bid the most. *Ramayan* was saved from the scheduled mock Hindu *Antyesti* rite of the last sacrifice. If there were no bids, Harold would have tossed him into the bonfire.

Earlier, a London tabloid reported, "...a Miss Fay Falconer, through her exceptional ghost busting and exorcising skills, cleared Lord and Lady Trafalgar's manor house of all extra-normal traffic."

TWINKLE TOES

ASTRA EXTENDED HER FOOT, breaking a beam of light, activating the steam-powered foot caddy idling beside her bed. Every morning the servants fired up the foot caddy's boilers to have it ready at any time for her toilette and preparation for the day.

Astra's ongoing physical problems focused on her feet. She often engaged podiatrists, orthopedists, osteopaths, masseurs, and anyone she felt could relieve her foot pain by manipulating her toes, feet, arches, and connective tissue. Her recurring pain gave her the idea for her invention. The foot caddy was her brainchild.

Astra Friedleifsdottir, an Icelandic lady of leisure, was a petite, five foot four, wealthy Viking woman who held some nonconformist views. Like most Nordics, she valued her independence and would do anything to maintain it. Conversant in the North European languages and English, she graduated in 1882 from the University of Uppsala in Sweden, with a major in Fisheries Science.

An avid fisherwoman on Icelandic rivers for salmon and trout, she left catching codfish to her father. The family's fortunes came from the sea in the form of his codfish fleet. Although she had no ambition to go fishing with the fleet, she felt it necessary to know the family's business.

A crack shot with a rifle, she had taken a polar bear that sailed in on ice flows from Greenland; its pelt decorated the family den. During the summers, she vacationed in southern Portugal for its glorious sun. While at the university, she had become a naturist. Reykjavik's ninety percent cloud cover foiled most nudist sun worshiping opportunities.

Astra had George Attwater, a noted English engineer in London, England, manufacture the foot caddy to her designs. Her expectation of a finely tuned machine for both her own use and for marketing came together gradually. It took over a year for George to make the unit and all the components Astra wanted. She streamed design upgrades by telegraphic cable with specifications and adjustments to London. She always made it personal and told George, "We just have to add (whatever she suggested), it'll make it ever so much more useful." One week she suggested a variable speed foot massager, the next, a nail trimming element, the next, something else.

Astra's specifications stated it had to be sturdy, have an adequate compartment for silk hose, shoes, and a slipper tray. Additionally, it had to have water tanks, liquid soap emulsions, perfume, hydrating lotions, cuticle oil, toe-nail polish, liquid shoe polish, and a steam-driven fan. If that wasn't enough, the caddy needed foot vibrating, kneading ability, a foot rest, and articulated chamois-skin fingers for the foot-stroking component. On the face of the machine, Astra instructed that there be a programmable acupuncture deck, a hot-air drying system, a toe-nail trimming and painting system, plus a robotic brush for each color shoe. For another quadrant of the caddy, she specified it have the capability of both buttoning high-top shoes and eyelet lacing, including the difficult task of fashioning the finishing bow-tie.

When Astra's completed *Twinkle Toes* machine arrived by ship in Reykjavik, Iceland—its name and mechanism had been patented in both Iceland and England, and world patents applied for. It took four dock workers to load it onto the flatbed of a horse-drawn drayage wagon for transport to her manse.

Installed in her boudoir, she said to her butler, "*Eg get ekki ath bitha ath reyna path*" or, "I can't wait to try it." She gave it its endearing English name, *Twinkle Toes*, to appeal to a larger audience.

Astra gave the machine its trial run. She knew it had been tested

and retested in England, but it was hers, and she wanted it to be perfect for her and future customers. Inserting her feet into the working area of the machine, it began sequencing the cleansing, massaging, and vibrating phase. When this was over, she switched it into toe-trimming, cuticle-softening, moisturizing, sanding, oil, hot stone, and drying mode. Next, the foot caddy put on her silk stockings from the reserve bin. By choosing the appropriate buttons, slippers, buckle, button or lace-up shoes, their polishing and brushing could be decided. A few misadventures occurred, but with cables to and from London, adjustments made, *Twinkle Toes* became ready for advertising and mass marketing.

When Astra's acquaintances heard about the machine, some started rumors about her being affected by foot fetishism, foot particularism, foot worship or podophilia. All of which Astra rejected out of hand when such scurrilous rumors came to her attention. She dismissed it as mere jealousy or envy of her superior accomplishments. One woman went so far as to inquire if it was healthy for Astra to be so enthralled with her feet. She asked a prominent neurologist why someone would spend so many Icelandic kronor on such an object. The woman contacted Dr. Pritchett Ramachandarian, an eminent specialist with a Freudian bent. He suggested: "Your friend probably suffers from foot fetishism caused by the feet and the genitals occupying adjacent areas of the soma-sensory cortex, possibly entailing some neural crosstalk between the two." This comment circulated in her small Reykjavik neighborhood of Grimmstathavoer by the sea, but in a less clinical fashion.

When Astra became aware of who was promoting these slanderous and hurtful rumors, she sent her distracters excoriating notes suggesting they should, among other things, work on their own personal problems and proclivities and leave her alone.

Eventually, Astra decided she'd had enough of these gossiping, billingsgate-tattling provincials. It was time to move on. Iceland had too many fishermen whose wives worried about the cod catch and not enough about the finer things.

Of course, Astra spoke English and knew Iceland was a limited market. She'd never sell many units of her invention in a country with only 70,000 people in 1890. She relocated to London to oversee the manufacture, upgrading, and marketing of her foot soother.

She formed a joint-venture partnership with George Attwater and subscribed capital for a manufacturing start-up, *Twinkle Toes, Ltd.* Ads were taken for the *TT Machine* in *The Daily Telegraph* of London and commercial newspapers on the continent. The machine soon became popular with the gentry who could afford this £25 luxury item.

Queen Victoria's footman heard of it and introduced it to the court. The queen found it so serviceable that she had one placed in each of her castles. Word also got back to Astra that her detractors in Reykjavik were also buying her units. They were no longer defaming her.

In time, Astra was called to Buckingham Palace for an audience and was subsequently put on the honors list and granted the honorary title of Dames Grand Cross of the Royal Victorian Order of the British Empire. Dame Astra went on to amass a fortune from her invention and married a Duke who loved having his feet attended by his own personal *Twinkle Toes.*

Still, for all her wealth and title, the Duchess of Thistlewaite, i.e. Astra, could be rankled when the tabloids continued to refer to her as the *Codfish Queen* when talking about her origins and fortune.

COVER STORY

THE AMERICAN ATTACHÉ at the United States Embassy in Paris heard a rumor of an aeronautical advance the French were working on, however, he did not have any specific details. He telegraphed Washington and told them of the tale. Word reached my editor at the Boston Globe, who called me into his office.

"Luke, have I got a dream assignment for you—Paree! You are going to Paris and report on scientific experiment presentations at the International Symposia. We also have a sub-rosa assignment for you which could be dangerous," he added. "You will also be investigating what the French are up to. Everybody is looking for aviation innovations and we can't let the frogs get ahead of us. We're depending on you to get the scoop."

He gave me the details and the date that I would sail, but neglected to mention it would be in 3rd class steerage accommodations, almost in the bilge of the ship. Once on board, I found out just what steerage in the late nineteenth century meant.

During the fifteen-day crossing of the Atlantic in the bottom of the ship, there was little opportunity to get up on deck. Ship's officers insisted we stay in our allotted class. Barricade chains were erected in the stairways between classes. Many of the passengers were rejected immigrants being sent back to Europe; others, were students taking the cheap way. Just to get a breath of fresh air from all the stench of the seasick, the crying babies and the foul body odors was an effort.

Finding a porthole to inhale the fresh sea air was difficult.

The bunks were tiered six high on the sides of the hull. Each canvas bunk in a steel frame was two and a half feet wide by six feet long with two and half feet clearance from the bunk above. Only an infinitesimal space was allocated for individual storage of personal items. The washroom had a single faucet, with open toilets only cleaned before docking. Stewards controlled our lives telling us what to do and when. Meals were hurry-up affairs with a variety of sliced liver, lentil soup, hash, salt pork, pickled herring, mutton, canned fish, along with potatoes, string beans, black bread and butter accompanied by weak coffee or tea. The canteen had apples, oranges, and candy if you couldn't stand the culinary fare.

Once in Paris, I hired Jacques Marchand, as a translator, since my French never amounted to much. A former soldier, he'd heard something about an experiment the French Army was doing, but thought that it was a state secret. He was certain it had to do with aviation with a new and unusual twist. Of course, this was what my editor wanted me to ferret out.

After I cabled my first report on the symposia that Oliver Wendell Holmes gave on his experiment to detect ferrous metals from the air, Jacques and I took a carriage back to Paris and repaired to *Le Fouquet* in the 9th Arrondissement on the Champs Elysees for dinner. I let Jacques pick the menu and we started with flutes of Perrier-Jouet Belle Époque Brut to wet the palate. Perusing the menu, he suggested an appetizer of calamari followed by a salad of shaved asparagus with aged gouda and hazelnuts. For the main entrée, steak tartar followed by Risotto Vert for a light entree topped off with Coupe Noire. With each course, another wine was chosen from whites through reds and topped off with a delightful dessert wine, an 1878 Chateau d'Yquem Barsac. Over the five-hour dinner, Jacques mentioned that he thought he knew of a way to find out about the covert project, without being too obvious.

"What's your idea?" I queried. "I still have a week before my ship leaves and we need to get on this. My editor will flog me if I can't come up with the information they want. If we can get some proof of what is going on, I'll have my critical second story."

He didn't respond immediately but suggested we take a walk. After dinner, we strolled through the Musee de l'Armee before closing hours. At the reception desk, he asked for a Sergeant Henri something or other in rapid French. Directed down the hall, we came to an office and I was introduced to Henri Duchasse, a former comrade of Jacques who was still on active duty. Invited to a local bistro for a vin ordinare or two, Jacques broached the subject with Henri about what the French were experimenting with in aeronauts. Henri too said he had heard rumors but didn't exactly know what was going on. He suggested we go to Reims, northeast of Paris, where the army tested its observation balloons, a most likely spot to find out.

Leaving from the Gare de L'Est, we arrived in Reims in the early afternoon. It was not difficult to find out where the army base was. We visited a few *bar a vins*, chatted up the locals and paid for a few *vin ordinare*, and voila! we had our answer. Off to Chatillon sur Marne, west of Epernay, outside of town we found it—an army airfield surrounded by a high fence.

We engaged a room on the second floor of a pension in the village and went down to the bar to again talk with the locals.

During the next few days, we strolled the countryside by the military compound. I brought along my Kodak No. 1 Brownie loaded with cellulose nitrate film and had just a few of the 100 exposures left. Pretending to take pictures of houses, carriages, and people, like a tourist, I only just pointed the camera. I had to save film since Jacques had used a lot of the film during my balloon ride with Holmes from my first assignment. I was waiting to discover this new device before using up any more precious film. We stayed within camera range of the army's testing field and kept it under scrutiny.

There were several observation balloons on static lines that went up in the morning and were hauled down at dusk. They had long hoses that pumped up hot air to keep them afloat. Through the gate on the compound grounds, we could see there were two large hot air furnaces used to inflate the balloons, and there was much activity to the whole enterprise. The locals speculated that they did this to train aerial observers should France have to go to war against the Boche, who were again saber rattling.

On the third day when we were riding rented horses to vary our routine, we saw in the airfield compound a most incredible dirigible being readied for flight. We had a better view because we were mounted and could easily see over the fence. "*Mon Dieu*," Jacques exclaimed, "*regardez ce monstre.*" An airship, at least 30 meters long with a steam boiler in the center began to rise after the hot air furnace had inflated its gas bag. I held up my Brownie and surreptitiously took a number of photographs. What was most unusual were the long cylindrical copper tubes attached to the dirigible's boiler. They were mounted on either side and there must have been 10 or 15 tubes, on both sides of the boiler, all pointing aft. Each was shaped like to an elongated milk bottle or an oddly shaped baguette. They were attached to the steam engine in the center, then tapered to half the original diameter towards the rear where they extended outside the basket.

As we watched, steam and black smoke roared out of the airship's stack as it ascended and set sail, heading east. We casually sauntered on our horses following the airship's route. Past the village and out into the open country, everything was quiet as the ship ascended until we heard a thunderclap and an increasing roar like the sound of a huge, high waterfall. We looked up to see the dirigible, moving not with the wind, but being pushed along by a current of steam issuing from the cylindrical tubes. It left a vapor trail that scattered the birds following the airship.

I looked at the Brownie's counter and saw I had only ten pictures left. I took the remainder of the roll to illustrate the steam locomoting the airship as it hurtled through the sky, propelled by the venturi effect through the cylinders. I had my scoop, a jet dirigible. If only the

Montgolfier brothers, the original balloonists, could see this.

In my cable to the Boston Globe, I encoded my copy with a cipher so the French wouldn't learn of my discovery about their secret ventures. For the text, I used an Atbash code, a substitution cipher where the letters of the alphabet are reversed—A is Z, B is Y, and so on. The code was easy to crack but good enough for my purpose. My headline read: ZNZARMT YZOOLLM GSFMWVIH LEVI UIZMXV. The Globe had the key and was familiar with it. We often used ciphers for reporting investigations when telegraphing our articles home, so the competition couldn't easily pirate the story.

Jacques said he was going to return to school, but this time to the University of Louvain in Belgium. I took a ship back to Boston and sent the Brownie camera to the Kodak company in Rochester, N. Y. A month later, I received it back reloaded along with the developed pictures we'd taken.

My newspaper revealed the French secret about their jet dirigible when my article was published, accompanied by pictures of it whizzing along. The French government made a formal protest through its ambassador to our government and to the newspaper, but nothing much came of it. Anyway, the cat was out of the bag. I also heard there were some bicycle manufacturers in Akron, Ohio who were playing around with a motorized airship. So, perhaps what the French were doing wasn't so important after all.

My biggest problem was the voucher for expense funds. When they saw the bill for the dinner Jacques and I had at *Le Fouquet*, 500 FF, and some centimes, they docked me the equivalent amount in dollars. My editor admonished me, "What were you thinking? Trying to make up for your steerage experience?" This admonishment was the result of my telegraph to him. I'd telegraphed and told my editor I was going to swim back if he didn't let me upgrade to at least second class on the way home, after mentioning the awful conditions in 3rd class. He agreed in a return telegraph. My protest that Jacques had done the ordering for that meal, that I couldn't read the menu and couldn't see the prices, didn't convince him, so I paid up—so much every week. But, it was worth it—the best damn meal I've ever had. And, it did make up for my ride in steerage on the way over.

I got raises over the years and my own column. During my life time, I reported on the first airplane crash, the first silent movie, President McKinley's assassination and many other world events.

UP THE RIVER

TWELVE OF US signed on to navigate the Demerara River in the heart of British Guiana, South America. We stopped at intervals to map the river along the traversable portions where streams or other rivers intersected. We expected to take our findings back to the Royal Geographical Society (RGS) in London for likely sugar cane plantation sites that could be established along the waterway. On board, we had a full complement of engineers, botanists, geographers, cartographers, porters, and several militia for protection.

In Georgetown, the capitol on the coast, we'd hired a guide, Jirol, who said he spoke most of the tongues of the indigenes. Unfortunately, it soon became apparent he was not up to the task and only wanted our money. During our first encounter with the natives, he made a show of talking their lingo, then the natives tried to kill him. We rescued him and ourselves and kept on going. We immediately became uncomfortable with this encounter and the savagery of the natives. Henceforth, we would be more cautious as we adventured upriver.

Our RGS expedition started hilariously at headquarters, where after too many brandies in early 1876, we concocted this new adventure. Now, six months later, after a seven-week crossing by sailing vessel, and a riverboat steamer from Georgetown, we worked our way up the Demerara.

Another local interpreter told us that no one should journey farther than Palemon upriver, as only death and destruction for white men could be found there. The locals in Georgetown suggested all the natives were hostile to outsiders and cannibalistic. When we tried to hire bearers, most of them left after they found out our destination. Finally, we engaged some coastal mulattoes as bearers, at an inflated price.

We brought trade goods: hatchets, knives, rifles, gun powder, beads, bolts of bright cloth yardage and bags of colorful buttons. Regardless of the admonitions to not go, we expected the natives to welcome us with our trade goods and help us out with our mission. Governor Young, the Crown representative, told us the natives did not like visitors. He explained that they had a deadly, poisonous powder they would sprinkle on interlopers. To overcome this threat, we made a huge steam-operated bellows connected to a rubberized airbag with hoses and a spigot gun. If anyone tried to powder us, one or more of us would man the high pressurized steam gun and fire hot salvos of steam against the invaders to repel the deadly powder. Meanwhile, the rest of the party would start shooting to defend us from the hostiles.

Of course, the natives are only one of the threats if you considered the other dangers found in the jungle from exotic animals and plants, for example: jaguars, black caiman, electric eels, red-bellied piranhas, green anacondas, bull sharks, pit vipers, assassin bugs, giant centipedes, common vampire bats, and a host of other creatures and insects. Depending on which you encountered, you could be eaten, crushed, stung, bit, weakened, and certainly you would wish you had stayed home.

Some of the plants our naturalist suggested we watch out for: angel trumpet, white snakeroot, belladonna, strychnine trees, wolfsbane, castor plants, crab's eye and many more. Just brushing against or ingesting one of these plants parts would ensure you'd never go home.

After traveling about 120 miles up the Demerara, we came under attack by poisoned arrows. Four of our members were killed outright. Arrows put holes in our bellows bag and all the steam fizzled away harmlessly. This attack sent the rest of us scattering for cover. Some hid in the boat, others jumped into the river and others ran into the jungle. Lord Harold Bloomingdale, our engineer, began to swim away from this hostile reception, then started screaming. Piranhas ate him alive. Nobody jumped in to try and save him, not even his valet, who scurried below deck.

The natives' attack came so fast and furious and so unexpectedly, we hardly had a chance to put our steam-gun into action. On top of which, it wasn't powder they sprinkled on us, but rather, an avalanche of spears and arrows that surprised us. Surrounded and captured, resistance seemed futile given the number of the war party. The fierce looking natives had bamboo skewers through their eyelids and noses. Clad only in loin cloths, they carried bows, arrow quivers, and lances, and menaced us with their weapons while taking us prisoner.

I didn't know what my captors were up to when they stuck several of us with their spear tips. Maybe, they wanted to see if we bled. We did—profusely, after several holes were punched in me and my fellow prisoners. Our bleeding appeared to be great fun according to their reaction. They giggled and shouted to one another like they had just captured some nice fat boars and verified blood pulsed through them. After that, I fainted. When I came around, I found myself depending from a bamboo pole, hands and feet lashed, being carried along. They'd bound me with jungle vines and hoisted me into the air for the trip, like I was one of the local marsh deer.

I found out why my back felt raw and stinging. When my bearers traversed over a hump, my back was dragged along the ground on the little hillocks before the ground leveled out again.

In the village, they threw me into a hut and took all my clothes. Now I was as naked as they were, except I felt ever more so. They'd taken my Saville Row boxers with little hearts on them my wife had given me. In any other environment, I would have felt extremely embarrassed being nude, but here, it was sheer terror. For two days I lay bound in the dark--no food, no drink and no clue what was coming next. I dreamed of my wife and children so far away and wondered

whether I would ever see them again. Delirium set in with a fever.
I passed out, awakening with chills, moving in and out of
consciousness. The downriver boys had it right—death for sure to
intruders. Where was my courage now?

In lucid moments on the third night, I looked through the loose
thatch of the hut and could see the tribe gathering around a fire. It
was a huge bonfire in the middle of the compound, flaming up as logs
thrown on it created a cinder shower of spectacular fireflies dancing up
from the impact. Tar torches lit the compound, and the natives were
moving in rhythm to drums that pounded out a beat reminiscent of
a tattoo from my old regiment, but much weirder. The music was a
call and response and it echoed out into the surrounding forest. Other
beats followed, sounding more like a xylophone with drum intervals.
During the musical intervals, I heard the natives jabbering away. I
wondered what they were up to besides getting ready for dinner. The
aroma from the fire reached into my hut and reminded me of roast
beef or pork with an acrid odor of burnt hair and a coppery metallic
malodor. I looked closer at the fire and saw a vision of my future or
that night's meal.

Our guide, Jirol, or his remains, dangled on a spit. Gutted, a
pastiche of leaves covered his feet and chest. A pole stuck through his
axis and bindings of liana held him tight to the pole. The ends of the
pole rested on two "Y" stakes on either side of the fire. Women at each
end turned the spit like a rotisserie rotating and basted him periodically
with some liquid. Every once in a while, it looked like one of the ladies
would also throw some kind of powder on him, because the fire, a coal
bed now, would sparkle and glow when the substance scattered and hit
the embers.

Looking away, I felt sorry for Jirol but not too much. After all,
he almost got us all killed during our first encounter with the natives.
Being isolated in the hut, I had no idea how many others of our party
remained or held captive, if any. If I was the only one left, would I be
next on the menu after they digested our guide? I didn't want to think

about it and immediately started making plans for my escape.

I'd sweated so much when I had the fever, the moisture eventually loosened the ties on my wrists and I easily tore the bindings off. Late that night I scrambled to make an opening in the back of the hut. Listening for sounds in the compound, I heard no noise and thought everyone was sleeping after their festivities. Squirming through my homemade back door, I crept to the river's edge, chose a pirogue beached there, gathered extra paddles and slipped into the river, lying flat in the bottom of the craft should anyone be watching. I quietly moved out into the downstream current.

Under better circumstances I would have looked for my companions. That thought didn't occur to me. It was either every man for himself, or for dinner.

It took days of canoeing and portaging, but I made it back to Georgetown, living off the land, finding fruit along the way. There was also fishing gear in the canoe I purloined and I put it to good use. To avoid traffic on the river, I holed up during the day to avoid any unfriendly encounters and paddled downriver at night.

When I reached Georgetown, Governor Young kindly put me up in a spare room in Governor's House. I idled my time on the beach, regained my strength and recovered from my wounds. It took three months before the next relief ship arrived and I was able to book passage for home.

One day at the market by the waterfront, I came across a native peddling his wares—shrunken human heads for sale. One looked familiar. It had golden blond hair, a full beard, and a dimpled chin. Inspecting it closer, I decided I had to have it. It was my expedition companion, Sir Ronald Babcock, our group's geographer. I'd bring him home to his wife.

This is a true account of our expedition to map the origins of the Demerara River in British Guiana. And, to seek and map potential plantation sites up to the river's headwaters for the Crown and the Royal Geographical Society expedition of August 1876.

THE SOPRANO AND THE MAESTRO

PENELOPE BRAXTON, aka Penny, a self-taught soprano, the lead singer in her church in Nottingham, left to find work and expand her opportunities. She came to London after saving her meager earnings as a shopkeeper. Arriving in St Pancras Railroad station on Euston Road from the Midlands, she detrained onto the twenty-year-old station built in 1868. The first thing she had to do was find a room she could afford and later share the rent with another working girl. Besides looking for work, she wanted to keep up with her music. She began soliciting all the churches of her Anglican denomination to see if they had an opening for a soprano in their choirs. She started with the largest churches in metropolitan London.

Her interviews had promise, but no serious offers were made to join any church or choir, even with testimonials from her home parish choir master and vicar of her church, St. Mary's. She was rebuffed over and over. Not for lack of talent, she was turned down because they already had a soprano, or had no choir, or she was not a member of their congregation; she was too young, not skilled enough, and many other excuses.

After weeks of searching for a choir position, it became necessary to concentrate on a job as her savings were almost depleted. Despondent with more rounds looking for work, she found herself frazzled after a day's search. Cooking a skimpy meal of fried haddock, toast, and tea, she decided to have a little fling and went to the Canterbury Music

Hall on Westminster Bridge Road. With a few pounds left, she was going to enjoy an evening of popular songs or whatever entertainment was being performed that night. After that, she'd go home, get a night's sleep and refreshed, continue looking for work.

At the music hall, she joined in on the choruses to such songs as *Glorious Beer, Waiting at the Church, Daddy Wouldn't Buy Me a Bow-Wow, Ta-ra-ra-boom-de-ay* and others. Between the singers, ventriloquists, knife-throwers, magic acts, juggling and plate spinning acts, she sang along, enjoying herself and a few pints. While waiting for the next act to begin, a woman sat down beside her and praised her singing. She explained she was a table away and heard Penny sing the refrain to one song or another.

"You don't mind if I join you, luv, do you? I heard your voice and it sparkles. Much better than that old dear that just fell on her face up there."

"Why thank you. Do sit," Penny responded.

"I bet you'd knock 'em dead if you got up there and belted out a tune. Wot say?"

"I'd be embarrassed. I've sung in choirs, but never in front of so many people. If they don't like your singing, they can be terrible."

"But you, I wouldn't worry. You'd hush 'em up and beer would be pouring your way," Penelope's new friend suggested.

After several pints, Penny, as she liked to be called, still sober as a church lady, went up to the maestro and requested a spot on the stage.

"You're up in 20 minutes, after the fire-eaters," he said.

"I'll sing a cappella," she replied, "so the band can take a break."

At her table, Penny reviewed the lyrics of her favorite popular song, *Runaway Girl*, and sang it softly to herself to be sure she knew all the words and the melody. Confident she could pull it off before this crowd, a cross-section of London's kippers and candelabra society, she took a swill of beer and headed for the stage at the maestro's cue.

The music stopped and the hall became silent as Penny went on stage. A few cat-calls came from the back. The drunks were amiable though, and there were the oft heard remarks, "Whatcha doin' afterwards?" or "Where's your old man?"

The maestro introduced her and her song: *Runaway Girl*. When he announced she'd perform without the band, there were some more hoots. Penny began.

"Hey there material girl,
The neighbors told me you're moving out
Leaving to witness the world
But are you sure that's what you're doing now..."

After the first stanza, they didn't let her go on with the next; instead, 200 or so voices rose up in the hall: "*So long, farewell... good bye, good day, be on your way, runaway girl.*"

Then, she went on to the end, but every stanza brought the house down and the audience pounded their mugs on the tables and sang the refrain. Exhausted at the end and thirsty, she returned to her table where mugs of beer were delivered in appreciation. When the next act went on, the maestro appeared at her elbow and introduced himself as Frederico Rizzoli. He chatted with her for a while and ascertained she was unemployed, looking for work. He made her a proposition.

"Miss Braxton, you're hired. I hope you are not afraid of heights. You're perfect for my contraption."

Taken aback at this possibility of a job, she said, "What is it?"

"I've a steam-driven rocket ship, guided by wires above the hall. You'll appear to drive it and when you reach the middle of the hall, it'll stop and megaphones will fold down around the ship. You'll do several songs, magnified by the megaphones, the lights will dim, and then you'll blast off, appearing to have gone into space, only, it'll be the attic."

"I hope you'll compensate me for this daring do?"

"Better than you could hope, five pounds a week."

"I accept," Penny said breathlessly. My ship has come in, finally, she thought.

ETAOIN SHRDLU

AROUND 1894, a young Gaelic speaking lad, Etaoin Cmfwyp, from the Irish Aran Islands immigrated to America, getting off the boat at Ellis Island. When asked what he could offer his new country, he replied in his native Gaelic language with a little broken English he had picked up on the crossing, the name for his old job, a *shaor cloiche*. Unfortunately, the officials didn't understand Gaelic and were unaware this meant "stone mason." They guessed he was a small animal herder. Looking at their list of possible placements, they immediately found vacancies out west and put him on another ship that took Etaoin around the Horn to San Francisco, California.

A sheep rancher, alerted by Immigration, picked him up at the docks and put him on a coach to Modoc County on the California/ Nevada border where the rancher had vast flocks of sheep but few herders. Etaoin found the high country similar to those at home but without the blustery gales and nearly constant rain of his native coastal Ireland.

Given a herd of sheep, a pittance of a salary, a walking stick and provender for the duration, he was assigned a large section of highland for the sheep to graze on for the summer. A small wagon situated on his turf became home. Fortunately, the ranch owner also gave him two trained herd dogs who seemed to know what to do better than Etaoin.

All the negotiations with Etaoin had been in hand gestures and pantomime. From this, Etaoin, thought he was to build stone fences for the sheep while the dogs were to be in charge of the herd. This was OK with him. He was back in his element, building corrals and fences from fieldstone and telling the dogs in his strange dialect to look after the sheep.

Meanwhile, a young Basque lassie, Extre Shrdlu, a daughter of a nearby sheep rancher, was told by her father to take their herd to the mountains for the summer and tend them. After months of lonely sheep herding and yodeling Basque Euskadari songs of love and longing in her native tongue, she yearned for company and companionship. Months in the bleak hills, with just the tinkling of sheep's bells for company, made her lonely. One day she heard strange, plaintive singing coming up from a nearby hollow:

> *Sheolfainn fein gamhna leat, Eibhlin a run*
> *Sheolfainn fein gemhna leat, Eibhlin a run*
> *Sheolfainn fein gamhna leat, sios go to Tir Amhlai leat*
> *Mar shuil go mbeinn I gcleamhnas leat, Eibhlin a run*

> *(I would herd calves with you, Eileen my love*
> *I would herd calves with you, Eileen my love*
> *I would herd calves with you, down to Tir Amhlai, with you*
> *Hoping to be matched with you, Eileen my love.)*

This strange music was in a language she had never heard before. It was also accompanied by the bleating of a large herd of sheep. She knew it was no echo of her own songs or her animals, but listening closely, she could feel the same plaintive undertones of her personal loneliness in this strange language resounding off the hills.

She decided there was someone over the hill that felt the same way she did and the way to meet him would be to sing back. Hardly waiting for his song to end, she began hers as loud as she dared, so he would hear her.

> *Zatoz nire lagun on orain heldu eskotik*
> *Dezagun larrak ze harkatzu txoriak bezala*

Eta kaka butuak horiek gustiak inoiz gustuko dugu
De zagun zabaldo eta lumadun hegal bat bezala dantzen
Txisto abesti; hao txuri aske bat abesten
Hode i batek gu re ezk ontza ohe gauean izango da

(Come on my friend now take my hand
Let's fly like birds across this land
And dump on all these heads we never liked
Let's spread and swing like a feathered wing
Whistle this song a free bird sings
A cloud will be our wedding bed tonight, tonight.)

When she ended, she listened but only heard the bells of both herds and their rustling feet as they came towards each other.

Etaoin had been singing his plaintive song while both tending the herd and looking for fieldstone. He told the dogs to corral the sheep and hold them while he followed the strange sounds. By this time, the dogs had begun to understand his hand gestures but not his words. They rounded up the sheep and kept them still. Walking towards the beautiful voice, he found Extre and in mime, introduced himself. Fortunately, Extre spoke English and talked to him in that language. He understood a little, remembering what he had picked up on the ship, and said, "How do you do?"

They met every day and he invited her to his camp. Gradually, they were able to communicate as Etaoin learned more English from her. No longer lonely shepherds, they became friends, then lovers. At the end of the summer, they brought their sheep down from the highlands and were married in the village.

They had a child who they wanted to name after themselves— Etaoin Shrdlu. Unfortunately, the child was polycephalic, a two-headed baby. They named one head Etaoin and the other, Shrdlu. Etaoin, who was the right side head, was enormously gifted with right-brain creativity and imagination. The left-side head, Shrdlu, was gifted with

extraordinary powers of logic, analytics and mathematical skills.

As the children grew up, Etaoin and Shrdlu astonished whoever came in contact with them with their respective intellectual capacities. Etaoin was a skilled, creative artist and thinker while Shrdlu was a world-class physicist and mathematician. Somehow, as they grew up, each switched off like a light bulb when the other was working on a project so the work would be finished.

Unfortunately, no one would hire them until they were discovered by the Barnum and Bailey Circus where they became a famous act. They could answer any question put to them by an audience including the origin of the name: Etaoin Shrdlu.

As a sideline, Shrdlu set type for the circus newspaper and Etaoin edited it. After many years with the circus, Shrdlu's head died but Etaoin stayed vital and in time absorbed all of Shrdlu's head and intellect into what was formerly their body. He became one head, one body, one person.

No longer dependent on the circus freak show for employment, Etaoin went on to become a famous anthropologist who tracked down cultural anomalies, particularly etymological ones, sometimes finding that important clues, were after all, only nonsense. And, just for the heck of it or to commemorate his parents and his brother and himself, Etaoin gave the name "Etaoin Shrdlu," to an absurdity; i.e. the unintelligible utterance. For this too, he became quite famous and went into the language and literature. The term can be found today in the Oxford English Dictionary.

In 1950, Etaoin was accidentally killed. He was driving, high on words, when he was blindsided by an 18-wheeler loaded with Campbell's Alphabet Soup.

DAY SAILING

HARRY BURTON, ENGINEER, bounded across San Francisco Bay in his experimental cutter-rigged sailboat under auxiliary steam power. The waves repeatedly struck the bow in soft blows as the hull plunged into the white caps on this blustery day. The wave crests parted in sparkly foam as the hull nosed forward, the craft motoring across the bay with the sea lions and harbor seals bobbing up to see who was out in their pond.

Harry was feeling ill, a sour stomach, a lightness in the head, disorientation, as the boat bounced and caromed with the waves; part sailboat, part steamboat bashing the surf. He'd eaten raw ginger to keep the sea sickness at bay, but it wasn't working. Even his girlfriend, Myrtle, steering the boat with the tiller in the transom seat was starting to become nauseated.

Harry had wanted to show Myrtle his transformative sailboat, a conversion from ordinary sail to a combination of scoop-sails and steam power. Myrtle, more a landlubber than a sailor, but enamored of Harry, went along for the ride. She was not sure how it would turn out but brave enough to go to sea at least once and show him she was a good sport.

Mid-bay, Harry throttled back the steam engine, disengaged it from the propeller drive shaft, and locked onto the belt-driven steam turbine that drove the rotating masts. On deck, he hoisted his newly sewn scoop-shaped sails to the boat's fore and aft masts.

Harry had spent hours making miniature models of his new type of sail and tested it on a small pond with a rubber-band engine to spin the spars. They worked filling out the scoops, billowing full and rotating on the miniature mast of his model boat. The scoops each had a large mouth and a small opening opposite to spill the air out. When rotating, they filled out and had the effect of pushing the craft forward. The experiment on the pond only lasted as long as the energy supplied by the rubber bands.

No longer running under propeller power, Harry's new sails were now ready for their trial run. To relieve Myrtle of steering, Harry locked the tiller with stays to keep the boat on a true course, then went below deck.

In the boiler room, his fireman, Joao, was shoveling coal to keep the boiler's steam pressure up for the trial. Harry was checking to make sure they were at maximum pressure before he started the run with his new sails.

"She's at the maximum, 50 psi," Joao said. "I've got her pegged and ready."

"Keep her there," Harry said, "When I signal, throw the lever to the turbine spur-gear that drives the belts for the masts. I want them spinning like a top."

Leonardo Da Vinci's drawings were Harry's initial inspiration for his invention, but as an engineer, he had his ideas he wanted to try out. He had a chandler on the waterfront negotiate the making of his unique sails. They were three vertical scoop sail sets for each of the rotating masts, each with a stiffener boom affixed to the top and bottom to keep them extended as they rotated and caught the wind. The rotation drove the boat forward without yawing with tiller support to keep headway.

Returning topside, he told Myrtle to hang onto her bonnet, as he was going to open the throttle and get the masts moving. He signaled Joao to throw the gear. Gradually, he inched open the throttle until the boat rose from the waves and started to plane over the white caps. The steam turbine spun the masts and sails and pushed the craft forward.

Harry Burton had spent a lot of spare time trying to decipher Leonardo da Vinci's backward writing to see if he could get some insight into the artist's way of thinking, and be as creative as he was. He took Italian lessons and mastered the 15th century idiom while in the California gold fields.

He designed his version of a long tom sluice to winnow gold out of the dirt, clay, and gravel of the mountain rivers of the Sierras. A team of Italian immigrants worked the gold with him. After a day's work, he'd gather his crew around after dinner and practice his Italian. The babble of the crew was in many different dialects. This polyglot jibber-jabber wasn't helpful. Harry knew that Leonardo was a Florentine and his crew spoke a jumble of Milanese, Venetian, Romanesco, Florentine, Neapolitan and Sicilian. Harry focused most of his language practice with the Florentine, Luigi Bartolo. He became fluent but knew he had to also learn written Italian. The gold field weren't the place to do it. He decided to quit his studies and concentrate on mining as much gold as he could.

After two years of mining and sending his earnings to the bank, Harry paid off his crew, shook the dust from his mining togs, and went to town—Sacramento. It was the jumping off place of many miners for the gold fields. Harry became a shopkeeper.

Always observant, Harry had noted how much he was making sluicing for gold versus how much merchants were charging miners for all the needed food and materials to stay in the field. They were hardly working, yet made more than the miners. They had inflated prices for staples: flour cost $50 for 100 pounds, beef $35 for 100 pounds, 16 cents for a pound of coffee, salt pork $75 for 100 pounds, wood $20 per cord and timber, $150 per 1,000 board feet.

He knew from experience that if a stream bench was any good, panning and sluicing brought in $40 to $120 a day. If the gold wasn't there, the miner had to move on and stake new claims or buy existing ones. Now that he had a grubstake, he figured he'd join the real money makers.

Harry rented a storefront on "K" Street in downtown Sacramento and bought his first supply of mining equipment, shovels, pickaxes, pans. He also stocked his patented long tom sluice, handguns, ammunition, knives, gravel rockers, hammers, nails, timber and other sundries. He was ready to cash in. In six months he did very well, until he noticed another trend.

Financiers were moving in and supporting immense mining operations that required large capital. Gigantic hydraulic mining rigs were taking over from the little guys. The pick and shovel and pan miners were dwindling just as the "easy gold" was drying up.

Harry saw the future, sold his business, and moved to San Francisco to open a general hardware store to cater to the growing metropolis. He established a "going business" on Market Street in 'Frisco town. Once he was profitable, Harry picked up a hobby.

He joined the local yacht club, found new friends and mined them for suggestions about which type of boat to sail. Harry liked to sail San Francisco Bay to the upper bay through Carquinez Straits, Suisun Bay, up the Delta and the Sacramento River. The vessels he rented were all too small to do any serious ocean sailing. Eventually, he found and bought his cutter-rigged unit that could handle coastal sailing and more.

A diligent, serious man, he also continued to improve his sailboat and his sailing abilities. Harry started to come in first for his class on most of the sailing races at the Corinthian Yacht Club, where he was a member. Not satisfied with just wind power, he speculated on how he could add steam power to his boat that would assist the sails.

With the throttle set to medium speed on this windy day, and his new sails working admirably, Harry decided to speed up, increasing the turbines rpm's and the revolutions of the masts.

Advancing the throttle, the yacht accelerated, and the masts spun. He decided to push it all the way for this trial expedition. When he pushed the throttle to the maximum, he could hear the roar of the turbine as it took hold at its highest speed. The belts spun the masts, and the sails drove the boat. The cutter jumped with the increase in speed and rocketed across the bay towards Angel Island.

"Myrtle," he yelled above the wind, "hold on to the tiller and keep her straight. I don't know what would happen if we changed course."

Myrtle held on for dear life. She'd never been much for boating, and this felt like a mechanical demon running hell-bent for leather across the bay. She was scared, but frightened or not, she wasn't about to let loose of the tiller or allow the boat to turn or go in any direction except straight ahead. She thought if she was a real sailor she should say, "Aye, Aye, captain." Instead, she shouted, "Take me home Harry! This is not what I signed up for."

Harry ignored her. Caught up in the moment, he was extremely anxious. He wanted to see how the craft ran, how the sails held up and if he had enough steam to make a good trial run. He knew he should be more solicitous. He didn't want to lose a girlfriend and a good deckhand—not now. This was too exciting a challenge, with new sails, a new invention, and a new girl, now was not the time to stop.

As the cutter-rigged unit accelerated, the scooped canvas sails drove the boat faster and faster. When a rip tore through the sails, flapping them into shards with a roaring sound, tattered canvas particles flew into the air, scattering in the wake of the boat. Rigging lines followed, flailing about the boat.

Harry and Myrtle crouched for safety in the open well of the cockpit. The vicious rigging tackle was whipping the air. Hugging the deck in the cockpit, they watched as rope, pulleys, and snaps wrenched loose from the masts and shot-gunned the surrounding waves. Then, the masts accelerated and spun unencumbered by the scoops until they reached the maximum rpms set by the turbine's governor.

Myrtle, frightened by the explosion of ragged sails popping and flying off the boat, sat frozen, holding the tiller. She was ready to cry and wanted to go home but couldn't move. Harry was shocked and could do nothing as he watched the sail cloth fly away. The boat was

losing headway. He didn't touch the throttle, just let the masts spin and throw off the last remnants of cloth and hardware. Then a strange thing happened. The boat should have come to a stop, but it didn't. When all the sail powers forward motion had died away, the vessel still proceeded towards the island. How come? The cutter continued to move about five knots an hour.

"Myrtle, loosen the straps, turn the tiller to port. We are heading home. We're witnessing an astonishing thing. A new form of motive power. The spinning masts are driving us. Not fast, but they are driving us. This is a eureka moment."

Myrtle, not caring what was going on, thought Harry had instructed Joao to engage the propeller, and that was what was taking them home to the yacht club. She couldn't wait to get off this death trap. If it was moving, no matter how, she was happy. Home was in sight.

Back at the yacht club, Harry told some of the members of his new idea of spinning masts and they scoffed at him.

"If you come up with spinning cylinders to drive your boat, we're going to blackball you. This is a club for motor and sail, not spinning tops."

Harry was unfazed by the criticism. He asked Joao to clean up the boat and get ready for a new trial. When Harry dropped Myrtle off in the carriage driveway of her home, he asked,

"Would you go sailing with me again?"

"Harry, you can pick me up anytime, but I'm not going out in your crazy boat again until you figure everything out. Then, maybe."

Happy to hear he hadn't scared her off completely, Harry knew he had to get back to his little pond with a model boat with thick paper rolls, lots of tough vulcanized rubber bands and time to prove out what he'd just witnessed. Maybe, the speed could be increased with more surface area on the cylinders? His thought was that the rotor masts driving the boat had something to do with Bernoulli's theorem and fluid dynamics.

BILL LYNAM. A lifelong reader and writer, he taught adult education for 30 years in New York while writing text books, short stories, travel, memoir, non-fiction, video scripts, poetry, and newspaper articles. In his spare time, he is working on a novel. Bill and his wife, Maria, live in Prescott, AZ.

RUSS MILLER. Scribbles were provided for this book by Russ Miller. He is a syndicated cartoonist and writer, having worked for Disney comics, Marvel occasionally, and many others who threw some coin at him. He is the originator of Russ Miller's Oddly Enough, and has been seen recently in a kilt playing bagpipes. A motorcycle enthusiast, angler, and commercial artist, he is surrounded by a menagerie of pets, livestock and one bitchin' redhead.

www.ingramcontent.com/pod-product-compliance
Lightning Source LLC
Chambersburg PA
CBHW050829180626
46814CB00004B/1521